LOOK AT ME!

FELIX BARON

Mischief
An imprint of HarperCollins*Publishers*
77–85 Fulham Palace Road,
Hammersmith, London W6 8JB

www.mischiefbooks.com

A Paperback Original 2013

First published in Great Britain in ebook format by
HarperCollins*Publishers* 2012

Copyright © Felix Baron 2013

Felix Baron asserts the moral right to
be identified as the author of this work

A catalogue record for this book is
available from the British Library

ISBN-13: 9780007553174

Find out more about HarperCollins and the environment at
www.harpercollins.co.uk/green

CONTENTS

Chapter One

A week back, Constance had caught Jeff rubbing pumice over the pads of his fingertips. Their eyes had met. His had been mildly amused. Hers, she felt, must have been both bewildered and excited. She hadn't been puzzled. She could guess why he was doing that. It was pretty obvious. He was smoothing the tips of his long artistic fingers to make them more sensitive to the texture of her skin. How was a good girl supposed to react to that? Intrigued? Complimented? Offended? What was appropriate? Life, and love, could be very confusing.

Now they were in bed together and she was reaping the full benefit of his smoothing. Jeff had a touch that was so delicate it felt like talcum powder was being sprinkled on her skin. Sometimes she couldn't tell whether she was actually feeling it or just imagining that she felt it. It was tantalising – maddeningly so. She loved it so much that she couldn't stand it.

Felix Baron

He was tracing lazy curlicues around her navel. She tried to imagine the sensations his fingers would be feeling, but failed. Instead, she concentrated on what *she* was feeling.

The meandering circles became ellipses that dipped further with each slow circuit. Constance held her breath. He brushed the edge of what he called the peach fuzz that coated her mound. That tickled.

If only he'd move lower!

But Jeff was taking his time. He always took his goddamn time! Sometimes she wondered if he did that to punish her for the one thing she refused to do for him, but that couldn't be. Jeff loved to please her. When he teased, it was just to make her pleasure more intense. She liked to make his pleasure more intense, too, except for doing that one thing. Apart from that, she denied him nothing. That thing was a biggie, so she had to make up for it the best she could.

The one thing that she wouldn't do for him was also, Jeff said, irrational. Well, maybe it was. She couldn't help that. It was due to her upbringing.

He was cupping her, taking command of her sex.

His palm covered her mound. His fingers were curved down, over her sex, resting on its delicate pulpy outer lips. She moved her thighs further apart to accommodate his exploration. His fingers palpitated, pressing in a steady one, two, three rhythm. Constance could feel herself moistening. One fingertip was on her sex's left lip, one on her right, and the other, delicately, so, so delicately, rested on the wrinkled crease where the lips met. The outer two fingers spread, parting her a fraction. The middle one curled down into her soft wet heat.

Constance groped sideways, into the fly of the pants of the pyjamas she insisted he wore to bed. Her fingers wrapped his hardness, not as a caress, but just for something solid to hold onto.

She was wet inside. She was so wet that it felt as if his middle finger was dabbling in a puddle of her juices. Almost splashing. And it wormed higher, insinuating itself up behind her pubic bone. Jeff'd told her that there was a soft dimpled pad there that he loved to massage. She loved it too. When he did that ... Oh yes! Just like that.

And now his other hand was working its fingers under his cupping palm, searching out her little button and finding it. Her lover's hands worked together, both rotating fingertips, one on her special place that was so deep, the other caressing her other special place, the one that was nestled just between her lips, where they joined.

Constance couldn't think. She barely remembered to breathe. The gyrating fingers were winding something inside her up, tighter and tighter and tighter. She reached the point where she could imagine no greater disaster than that those fingers should stop what they were doing before she got to where she was rushing ...

'Don'tstopdon'tstopdon'tstop!' That was her, babbling, wasn't it?

'I won't, I promise,' Jeff whispered.

The glorious thing happened. Ecstasy rippled through her. Constance's thighs drew up to her chest, spread wide. Her hips came up off the bed, paused, then slammed down. Spasms convulsed her.

After a crystalline moment of sheer bliss, she returned to her senses. She let her legs drop back to the sheet. Oh yes, she was holding onto Jeff's cock, wasn't she.

From a dark recess in Constance's mind, her dead mother started to scold her for thinking such a word as 'cock'. That was OK. It was when Mom reviled her for showing too much skin that she couldn't stand it.

Dreamily, Constance turned to Jeff and told him, 'That was wonderful. What can I do for you, darling?'

'Turn over, Connie.'

Oh! She knew what that meant. He was the first and only man who'd ever done *that* to her. Her mom had never warned her against it, most likely because she'd never imagined such a thing. It was certainly never mentioned in the *Book of Chaste Behaviour* that her Mom's puritanical sect considered second only to the *Ten Commandments*.

Whatever, her mom wouldn't be scolding her and spoiling Jeff's, and her, pleasure.

Constance rolled onto her tummy and tensed, waiting. He was above her, poised for a second, and then he lowered himself onto her like a warm and heavy blanket of love. His weight was mainly on his knees and elbows but even so, it was inexorable. She was deliciously helpless, even before his fingers wrapped her wrists and the insteps of his feet nestled into the arches of hers. If she could move an inch, it was only because he allowed her to.

The heat of his cock's stem spread into her spine from her tailbone to the small of her back. Feeling the length of it thrilled her. Even though he'd taken her, used her, that way before, what she knew he was about to do had to be impossible. She was so small. He was, by comparison, huge. Where he was going to enter her, it was a tight little knot. His cock – its head in particular – was far too big. Dreadfully big.

When was he going to do it? What was he waiting for? She couldn't ask for it, could she?

The hidden minx inside her told her that she could.

Constance moaned, 'No, Jeff! Please, don't. Don't do that. I don't know if I can stand it.' The cheeks of her bum flexed but all they could feel was his scrotum. She tried to work herself higher up the bed but his restricting bulk made that impossible.

Jeff whispered, 'You'll take it, Connie. I am going to make you take it.'

'You are going to force your way into me back there, with that great big *thing*?'

'Yes, darling. I am.'

'That's *so* bad.'

'And you love it, don't you?'

'Do I?'

'Admit it. You want it.'

He was torturing her. He knew about her upbringing. He knew how strict her mother had been. He knew that she hated to own up to her own perverted desires. Hated to. Loved to, if forced to. It had to be forced from her or she wouldn't – couldn't – do it.

Would it be the same with the other thing, the one thing she refused to do for him? If he forced her, would she find that she liked it? No! Don't think about that. Thinking that way was dangerous. It woke memories of her dead mother's rules.

Constance hollowed her back, tilting her bottom up at him.

'Good girl! That's right, just like that!' Without releasing her, Jeff slithered back and lower, drawing his shaft down along the crease between her cheeks. He prodded. It wasn't the right place, too low. Last time, he'd steered himself with a hand.

As if he'd heard her thought, he told her, 'Hands free, this time.'

Constance grunted.

Jeff writhed an inch each way and up and down, probing.

Yes!

The wet hardness of his knob was nestled right against her trembling pucker, kissing it. He pushed. Constance pushed back. If she concentrated on relaxing back there ...

Oh. Oh. He was stretching her. He was forcing his way into the narrow constriction. Constance felt herself expand. It didn't hurt, not much, but it was such a violation of her tender flesh.

And he was inside her.

Just the head. Her muscular ring gripped his cock just behind its dome. The moment, the brief second of maximum stretching followed almost instantly by a partial relaxation, had been exquisite. It was like some sort of revelation.

Perhaps he read her thoughts again because Constance felt his thigh muscles tense and then the reverse pressure as he drew back, almost dragging the sleeve of her rectum with him, and 'popped' out ...

And rammed back in.

This time there was no pause. His thrust went on and on, opening her depths, forcing her back passage to adapt to the shape and girth of his shaft. Jeff's pubes were grinding on her as if he was desperate to gain every last possible inch of penetration. And he was pumping. Each stroke felt easier than the one before and yet her excitement grew and grew.

His big hands took hold of her hips. Jeff knew not to pull her up to all fours – she didn't allow that, just in case it dislodged the bedclothes – but he heaved her up off the bed just a few inches before slamming back down on her. She was totally impaled.

He half-rolled, so that her weight was on her left side. His right hand worked under her. Its fingers found her button again, but toyed with it for just a second before they squirmed past it, inside her. Jeff must be able to feel his own shaft pistoning into her. That was so obscene.

It was the obscenity of it that drove her over the edge into the chaos of her second glorious climax.

It must have been three or four in the morning when Constance woke up. It might have been the dim light from the small lamp on the bedside table on Jeff's side. It might have been him folding the bedclothes down to her waist and fumbling with the buttons at her throat.

Damn!

Constance sat up sharply, clutching the neck of her nightgown. 'No!'

'Please, Connie? Surely …'

She slapped his face and turned over to bury her face into her pillow. The bed creaked as Jeff got up. He'd be headed into her living room to finish the night on her lumpy couch. Well, she wasn't going to be guilted into doing something she didn't want to do. Let him suffer!

Chapter Two

When Constance woke again, with the first light, Jeff still hadn't come back to bed. Men! As if sulking solved anything. She decided that she'd take the moral high ground and simply pretend that nothing had happened. If he apologised, all to the good. If not, well, she'd just have to forgive him anyway. That was the way women were, forgiving and modest – sweet and modest – charitable and modest. Always modest. Modest. The damn word landed with a dull thud.

He wasn't on the couch and it hadn't been disturbed. There were no dishes in the sink. His shaving gear and toothbrush were missing from the bathroom. His spare suit wasn't in the closet. There was a space on her bookshelves where his IT books had been.

Jeff had taken his things back to his own apartment.

She'd been dumped. Well, no. She'd dumped him, really. A slap across the face counts as that, right? He'd broken her rule. She'd slapped him. He'd left, taking his things. How did she feel about that? Crushed, for sure.

Empty inside? Maybe. She'd thought he might have been the one. Angry? Yes, she was angry. How dare he! Look at all she'd done for him, the things she'd let him do to her. For him, she'd been a very bad girl. She'd enjoyed it all, but that was beside the point. When a girl does those forbidden things for a man she's doing him a favour, no matter how good they feel. All she'd ever denied him was to let him look at her shameful nakedness. Could that be so important that it'd make him break up with her?

Couldn't he have explained that?

Perhaps he'd tried, but not hard enough, obviously. The bastard!

What was it about the sight of a girl's body, anyway? She'd let Jeff bugger her. Bugger, bugger, bugger. Bugger her. Fuck her up her bum. *There!* If he'd wanted a bad girl, she'd been the baddest, for him. He'd been ready to risk losing *that*, just for a chance to look at her naked? It made no sense at all.

Why were men so obsessed with looking at women's bodies?

On a whim, very quickly, before the impulse fled, Connie sat down in front of her dressing table, slipped the top three buttons of her cotton nightdress and smoothed it down her right shoulder and breast – all the way, not just exposing its upper slope but baring it completely, nipple and all. By reflex, her eyes flinched away but she forced herself to actually look at her own smooth pink skin.

It wasn't as if she'd never seen a breast before. When she'd first left the commune, it'd seemed that she couldn't open a magazine or watch TV without them jumping out at her. Seeing and looking are two different things. Her mother had trained her to avert or close her eyes when they were exposed to immodest displays. It was hard. In the outside world, girls wore skimpy or transparent tops all the time, and not just in special places, like beaches, that could be avoided. They also displayed their legs in most unseemly ways. Her mother had allowed that exposed calves were acceptable. Not knees, though. Nor anything higher. Certainly not!

Well, there was her bare right breast, in the mirror, and she was looking at it.

In a way, it was a disappointment. Not because it wasn't pretty. It was. Her skin was so pale a pink that it was almost translucent. She could just make out a delicate blue tracery below the surface. Her nipple was a crinkled berry, darker than its halo, but not by much. As for shape, she felt she could compete with the statues she'd seen when Jeff had dragged her to the museum to demonstrate that he was right and she was wrong.

How was it that she didn't find the sight of her own flesh exciting?

Somehow, Connie had been sure that if she exposed herself that way, to herself, there'd be a forbidden thrill. There wasn't. Not exactly. Maybe a twinge? How about if she imagined that it was someone else's breast, Shirley's, the office receptionist's, for example?

Maybe she felt something. Just a pleasant little buzz?

Is that all there was to it? Why had Mother made such a fuss? Come to that, why had Jeff been so obsessed? It was his silliness that had broken them up. She'd like to ... make him suffer! That's what she'd like to do, and if she dared, she knew exactly how it was she could make him squirm.

For a moment, Constance considered touching her nipple but decided against it. She'd looked at it. That was a good start. Perhaps the first time she touched herself there, it'd be under the bedclothes. Little by little ...

Towards what end?

Mother had liked to talk about the slippery slope. One little sin always leads to a slightly greater one, and so on, until you were damned to hellfire for eternity. Mom'd been right when it came to the physical acts. Connie had avoided being kissed until she was twenty but once she'd allowed a boy to put his tongue into her mouth, it'd been an exhilarating downhill ride, all the way down to sucking a man's cock and finally to allowing Jeff to force his up her bum. After that, there'd been a bit of disappointment. By then, she'd committed all the sins she knew of, except the one of physical immodesty. What next? Well, now she knew. She'd exposed herself, to herself. Next, she'd expose herself to Jeff, just a little, just enough to drive him crazy. And to make him feel remorseful. Eventually, if he begged nicely, she might consider taking him back.

She didn't dare, did she? Dare tempt Jeff? *That* way? Did she? It'd be the worst violation of her mom's rules possible.

If she was going to do it, she'd have to do it straightaway, before her courage failed her. When she went in to work, in just under two hours, it'd have to be dressed as the new and slightly immodest Constance, not as whatever it was that she had been up to now. A frump? A prude?

Constance's office 'uniform' was always a twin-set worn with a single strand of cultivated pearls, plus a straight skirt that went down to just below her knees. She had no alternative outfits, so she'd just have to see what she could do with what she had.

After forty minutes of experimentation, and feeling like a total hussy, Constance left her apartment with the waistband of her skirt rolled over twice, so that her hem just skimmed her knees, and wearing just the cardigan of her twin-set, *with no bra under it and with the top button undone.* She added a light topcoat. It wouldn't do to get arrested on her commute.

On the bus, a man gave her his seat. Did the sluttish way she was dressed show on her face, somehow? When she got to the office, hung her coat and turned, reluctantly, to face the population of her working world, Shirley smiled a welcome at her. That was new.

For a while, Constance worked with her elbows tucked in tightly but she gradually got used to her breasts feeling loose and free and forgot about it until Larry, the mail delivery lad, brought her some files. His eyes widened and he blushed. Constance glanced down at herself. Damn! A second button had come undone. She was showing two inches of cleavage.

That was terrible. She wasn't ready for such a blatant … Or was she?

If she was so shocked at herself, how come her cheeks were glowing? How come she felt so warm down there?

Larry shuffled. Constance looked at him and quickly averted her eyes. The lad was wriggling to conceal an erection – that she had caused. He was only a boy – barely nineteen. At his age, he most likely had an erection most of the time. Even so, his reaction, she had to admit, gave her a certain sense of satisfaction.

As he turned away, Constance put her hand to her throat to do the extra button up again, but decided not to. Making men horny was kind of fun, she'd discovered. Sorry, Mom!

At coffee break, Shirley was pouring herself an espresso. The curvy redhead looked Constance up and down thoughtfully. 'New boyfriend?' she asked.

'No. Why do you ask?'

'You've got a certain glow about you today, honey, like you've been fucked three ways from Sunday.'

Constance had forgotten the earthy way Shirley had of

14

talking when away from her desk. It should have shocked her but somehow she found it refreshing. 'I dumped Jeff,' she confessed. 'Perhaps that's it.'

'The cute IT guy? He any good?'

'Any good?'

'In bed.'

Constance felt her face burn. 'I guess. Yes, to be honest, he's pretty good.'

'Mind if I do him?'

'You mean …?'

'Fuck him. He's pretty cute, but if you'd have a problem …?'

'No, no, no problem,' Constance lied.

'Thanks. Say, Connie, you doing anything at lunch?'

'No, why?'

'I'm going to shoe-shop. Want to come along?'

What was happening? In five years, no one in the office had ever approached her socially. She knew that some of the other women, the younger ones mostly, got together to go places. She'd overheard some of them talking about going clubbing and the like. Constance had never been included. Now, just because she was showing a little cleavage, she was sure, she was being invited. How powerful was *that*?

'Sure, love to,' she said without stammering.

'One o'clock, then?'

'One o'clock.'

Chapter Three

Time was, when Constance would have been mortified to have walked down a busy street beside an over-made-up girl in a too-short skirt and too-high heels who swung her hips so emphatically.

To her own surprise, shame was the last thing she felt. So how did she feel? There was a trace of pride in being seen with someone who drew so many approving stares. Then there was jealousy. Constance might as well have been invisible, or, at best, a moon to Shirley's sun.

But she was prettier than Shirley. She knew that, even if the thought was immodest. She was prettier but she wasn't – sexier. That was it. And that was by her own choice, or by her mother's.

Damn you, Mom. Look at what you've deprived me of, all these years. Well, it ends, *now*! A sense of relief washed through Constance. She felt reborn, emerging as a liberated woman, free for the first time in her life.

Shirley said, 'If you've got it, flaunt it. I just caught

our reflection in a window and that's the thought that popped into my mind.'

'What?'

'It's my philosophy.'

'Oh!'

'Don't hide your light under a bushel, right?'

'Right.' Wow! Shirley could justify her brazenness with quotations from the Bible. With that justification, Constance tried swinging her hips a little. It took a moment to get the rhythm right but, once she got it going, it almost felt natural. Almost.

'Here we are,' Shirley announced. She led the way in.

The boutique was called *Spikes*. Constance swallowed hard. The shoes on display were ... impossible. But beautiful, in a dozen different perverse ways. There were sculptures in leather, scraps of fabric on soaring heels, straps that made Constance feel restricted just from looking at them, puffs of pink fluff and slivers of snakeskin. People actually *wore* these?

A tall thin man in lavender pants and a matching shirt waltzed up to Shirley and arced to kiss her cheek without making body-contact. 'Shirley-girly, my pet! How nice to see you again.'

He turned his head to give Constance's feet a pitying glance that made her want to hide them. To Shirley, he continued, 'For work or for play, today, my lovely?'

'For play.'

He giggled. 'Well, shoes *are* foreplay, in my opinion. What fun! New man?'

'No. That's why.'

'Good strategy. Four inches again?'

'And a half.'

'Well, that's progress at least. I'll get you up to six inches one of these days, you mark my words.'

'I'm sure that you will, but I don't want to tower over all the men.'

'There are many men that love to be towered over, Shirl. I'm tall but it hasn't hindered me.'

'They're not my type, Percy.'

'Different strokes.'

'For sure,' Shirley said. 'Shoes for clubbing, please, Percy. I've got two new outfits, one in liquid gold, the other in a silver mesh.'

The strange man disappeared into the stacks.

Constance whispered, 'What did you mean, "liquid gold"?'

'It's a fabric, very thin, very clingy, that looks like metal has been melted and poured all over you. It shows off your nips, and you can even see your bellybutton through it.'

'Oh!' Constance thought about that for a while, and about what it'd look like on Shirley, and on herself. Was she ready for something like that? Maybe not – not yet, anyway. Still, the thought of being seen in something so revealing made her feel a glow, down there. And if Jeff ever saw her in anything like that, he'd go crazy with desire, for sure.

Shirley put a finger on Constance's knee. 'Heels are very powerful. A woman can be old and fat and ugly but if her heels are high enough, men will still look at her *that* way.'

'You're kidding.'

'I kid you not.'

The shoes that Percy brought for Shirley to try had heels as thin and cruel as nails. The soles were like paper. The uppers were interlocking teardrops, one gold, one silver, and with gold and silver cord ankle straps.

'Are those strong enough to walk in?' Constance asked.

Percy's eyebrow lifted. 'If you're looking for "sturdy", you should try army boots,' he sneered.

Shirley tapped Constance's wrist. 'Apart from a little dancing, I won't be on my feet much in these. That's the whole point.'

Constance thought for a moment, then blushed.

Percy squatted at Shirley's feet. He lifted her left foot almost reverently, slipped her shoe off and eased a sandal on. One hand supported her arch; the other adjusted the ankle strap. Each movement was a subtle caress. When he'd repeated his actions with her other foot, he lifted them both to plant a pair of gentle kisses on the taut bows of her insteps.

Constance looked away and then back. It felt as if she was spying on lovers in an intimate moment. But she'd thought he was one of those 'gays'. It was very confusing.

Shirley told Percy, 'These are perfect. Your taste is exquisite, as usual. Now see what you can find for my friend, will you?'

Constance gasped, 'What?'

'You're transforming yourself, aren't you? A butterfly emerging from her chrysalis? Let's move the process along, shall we?'

'I didn't say anything about …'

'You didn't have to. One day you're a frump, the next day you look kind of pretty, and you aren't wearing a bra. Draw a line from one to the other, and what do we have?'

Constance folded a protective arm across her chest. 'What?'

'Eventually, a very cute little sexpot, that's what.'

'I don't know …'

'I do.' Shirley turned to Percy. 'Conservative, for this time, dearest. Black, I think, and three inches?'

'Does she have her learner's permit?'

'*Percy!*'

'Sorry.' He scuttled back into the stacks. He returned with a shoebox. 'Plain black pumps. What could be more conservative?'

Shirley told him, 'Help the girl try them on, then.'

'Love to, but ...' His disdainful look at Constance's scuffed loafers spoke volumes.

She kicked them off.

'Thanks, Shirley's friend. It's not that those dreadful things are actually contagious, but ...'

'You wouldn't want to soil your hands on them,' Constance finished for him.

He squatted. From down there, he might be able to look up her skirt. Constance clamped her knees together but he didn't so much as glance upwards. His eyes were on her feet.

'What cute little piggies,' he said. 'Poor things.' He looked up into Constance's eyes. 'They deserve better of you, you know,' he accused.

'Sorry.'

'There, there,' he told her toes. 'Percy will dress you up nicely. I'll be right back.' He took tissue paper from the shoebox and used it to pick Constance's loafers up and carry them away. There was the sound of something being dropped into a waste bin before he returned.

Shirley whispered, 'I know he's a bit eccentric, but he *does* know his shoes.'

Constance replied, 'I guess I have the choice of either buying a new pair or going back to the office in my stocking feet.' She grinned to show that she wasn't really upset. In fact, she was quite enjoying the strange man. She'd never before bought clothes from anyone who actually cared what she bought.

21

Percy returned and put the pumps onto Constance's feet with as much tender care as if he'd been wrapping Fabergé eggs. As his fingertips slid across the sensitive skin under her arches, she felt an answering subtle twitch of the tendons that run beside the hollows high on the insides of her thighs. The vamps were cut just low enough to expose half-inches of toe cleavage.

'Walk, please,' he announced.

Would she stumble and disgrace herself?

Shirley advised, 'Get your centre of gravity above the balls of your feet. When you walk, your toes go down first. Remember, one foot in front of the other.'

'You can do it,' Percy encouraged.

It was like having a cheering squad boosting her. Constance set her feet firmly, shifted forward and concentrated on the sensations her legs' muscles were feeling. It felt good – an elegant tension that rippled up her limbs.

And she was erect.

Constance took a short step, then another. Emboldened, she made the next one longer and stumbled but caught herself.

'You're doing fine,' Shirley told her.

'And now you are become a veritable swan!' Percy exclaimed. 'Look at what those shoes have done to your legs in the mirror. Pull your skirt up a tiny bit, there's a good girl.'

Blushing with pleasure, Constance pinched the fabric

just above her knees and lifted her skirt's hem a few inches. In the mirror, her ankles had become more slender, her calves fuller. There were dimples in her knees and her thighs looked shapelier than she'd imagined them to be – not that she'd ever given much thought to what her thighs looked like.

'Oh!' she said. In a rush, she added, 'Perhaps I'll take two pairs like these.'

'No,' Percy told her. 'That'd be a waste. Come back in another week and we'll try you in three and a half or even four inches. You'll take to wearing real heels in no time, I promise. You're a natural.'

'But she'll take three pairs of stay-up stockings,' Shirley said. 'Would you believe that she wears' – her voice dropped to a whisper – 'pantyhose.'

'Of course I noticed. I just didn't want to embarrass her by mentioning it.'

As Percy wrapped, Shirley gave Connie a quick lecture on how to sit to take advantage of her new look – ankles crossed neatly to the side, so demure, so enticing.

On the way back to the office, Constance got just as much passing masculine attention as Shirley did. It felt a bit like the time she'd got into her dad's hard cider, thinking it was just spicy apple juice.

She stopped by the ladies' room and popped another button at her throat. Jeff was way overdue to visit. Before they'd broken up, he'd paused at her desk at least once every other day. She couldn't wait to see how he reacted to the new Constance but she imagined he'd be stunned, then contrite, then desperate to get her alone to make love. When he did, she'd leave the lights on. Ha! What he'd see would devastate him, and in a good way.

And she'd see him. She'd see Jeff's naked body. How did she feel about that?

Jeff hadn't passed by her cubicle that day, not once. Still, he had eight floors of PCs to look after. Perhaps he was very busy. Perhaps he'd simply given up on her. She had to face that possibility. What if Jeff took up with Shirley?

Constance had a quick flash of her ex entwined with her new best friend, two lithe and lovely young bodies, undulating urgently.

No.

She hit Control 5 on her keyboard and brought the Andrew's Aircraft queue up. The screen was a bit misty but then she blinked and it cleared.

Chapter Four

Constance pulled her cotton nightdress over her head and down as far as her hips. She paused. Why did she have to wear that ugly old thing? Modesty? Hadn't she shed that? She yanked the offending garment up and off, tossed it into a corner, scurried into bed and slid deep under the covers.

Why the rush? So she wouldn't see herself bare? Was that how it was going to be? A constant battle between her newfound pride in her body and all those sad years of puritanical conditioning? She was not ashamed of looking at her own body, and she would prove it.

She always had a penlight under her pillow, just in case she had to get up in the night. Constance snuggled down with her knees up, making a tent out of her bedclothes, and turned the light on. The bulb was actinic, and gave a blue-tinted light that washed the colour of her skin out. The pinkness had disappeared, leaving her very white. It made her breasts look as if they had been sculpted out of pure snow. She cupped her left breast. It was soft but resilient, and very warm, almost feverish. Her nipple wasn't soft, though. It was quite hard. When she squeezed it between two fingers, it felt like rubber. A harder pinch made her gasp. A little tug drew pangs of pleasure from deep inside.

Jeff would have killed to watch her play with herself. He'd asked her for that but of course she couldn't do it for him, not back then. Now?

Even stimulated, her nipple was still snow-white in the flashlight's light. Somehow, it looked a bit evil – like the skin of a girl vampire in a movie.

She'd noticed that effect long before, though not in an appreciative way. She and her cousin Sarah had told each other ghost stories by the light of that bulb, shining it up under their chins to make themselves look scary. Once, Constance remembered, Sarah had put the bulb inside her mouth so that the light showed through her cheeks.

There was a thought. What would it look like glowing through the skin of her …?

Constance tucked her pillow up to elevate her head. Her knees came up higher and spread wide. Two very decadent fingers parted the lips of her sex. The lens of her penlight slipped in easily, as if she'd been lubricating. Perhaps she had. She pinched her lips closed just below the lens.

How pretty it looked!

Her skin was glowing from within her body, glowing pink now, not white. Her flesh must have filtered the ultra-violet out. She moved the light. The glow followed suit. She pushed it deeper. The glow faded, then brightened as she pulled it back. And faded. And brightened. And ... and ... and ...

Look at me, Jeff! Watch me fuck myself with a penlight! Look at me. I'm going to get there. I am. I am. I'm so close ... I'm ...

Oh! Oh!

That'd been nice. It wasn't quite like when Jeff had done it to her with his fingers, cock or tongue, but it was still very pleasant. That was an interesting lesson. While she waited to get back with Jeff there were ways she could cope with her growing need. She'd known that some girls got themselves off with their fingers, of course, and she'd try that, now that she was bad, like other girls, but she'd never considered using *things*.

Wouldn't Jeff be surprised when she let him watch as she diddled herself with a penlight!

27

Chapter Five

For the fourth time that Saturday morning, Shirley shook her head and told Constance, 'I don't think so.'

Constance pouted. 'Why not? Doesn't it look good on me?'

'It looks great. Very sexy.'

'Then?' Constance checked herself in the boutique's mirror. She'd never gone for a 'tailored' look before but it certainly worked for her. The minute she'd seen the trim little black-with-white-pinstripes suit in the window she'd known she had to have it.

'The skirt, for a start,' Shirley told her. 'It only just covers the tops of your stockings, and then there's a slit another three inches higher. The fit, for another thing. It *really* emphasises your shape.'

'So?'

'It looks like what it is, Connie, a whore's version of a business suit. It's "business" all right, but not the sort of business we're in.' She paused, looking

28

thoughtful. 'Connie, I've been meaning to talk to you about that.'

'About what?'

'You know I support you coming out of your shell, a hundred per cent. You've transformed yourself and I'm proud of you.'

'With your help.'

'Yeah, well, maybe too much of my help.'

'How do you mean?'

'You don't go out at night, not to clubs or the like, and the sorts of things you've been buying lately are designed for night-time wear. They might be a bit too sexy even for singles bars, unless you want to give people the wrong idea.' She bit her lower lip. 'What I'm saying is, there's talk around the office. You might have crossed the line in some people's eyes.'

'Crossed what line?'

'The one between "classy-but-sexy" and "scorching". Not that you look cheap, far from it. You look great – great enough that when you go to the water cooler, every man on our floor suddenly gets thirsty. How many of them have asked you out?'

'A few,' Constance confessed.

'But you've turned them all down? If you went on dates to clubs you'd have a chance to show off all you wanted.'

'I don't know if I'm ready for clubs and dates yet.'

'Still carrying a torch for Jeff?'

'Not exactly.'

'Then?'

'It's hard to explain.'

'You want the men to look but not touch, is that it?'

'Shirley, the old me, she isn't exactly dead yet. There's still a bit of a puritan inside me. The way I am now, well, I could pull back if I had to, retreat into who I used to be, dressed the way I used to dress. On the other hand, if I got into a relationship the way I am now, that'd make the new me the real me and bury the old me for ever. I'd be burning my bridges. Does that make sense?'

'Do I understand your words? Yes. Do those words make sense? No.'

'Well, I'm buying this suit, anyway.'

'But not to wear for the office, please?'

'OK.'

'Connie, you know what you need, apart from getting fucked good and hard and often?'

'No, what do I need?'

'To give the new Connie a test-run. See if you like her well enough to live with her, and without the old you.'

'How do you mean?'

'Find yourself a place to go where no one knows who you used to be. Be your new self there, complete with steamy relationships, if the right guys come along. Then, if it doesn't work out for you, you can retreat back here, where I'll be waiting to help keep you on an even keel.'

'That sounds complicated.'

'Nonsense! Next long weekend, take a mini-vacation somewhere where there's lots of action. That might be all you need to sort yourself out.'

'What if I fall for some guy who lives a hundred miles away?'

'That's something we'll just have to deal with if and when it happens. One problem at a time, please, but if it does happen, ask him if he's got a friend for me, right?'

* * *

On the following Monday morning, Constance got a call from Mrs Carey in HR. 'Connie, I'm making up the vacation schedules.'

'Yes?'

'You didn't take a single day last year, nor the year before.'

'So?'

'You'll have accumulated eight weeks, come June the fifteenth.'

'Eight weeks?'

'You're entitled. If you decided to take it all at once, it'd really make things difficult for me.'

'Sorry about that.'

'So, you have to use some of it up, soon, like two weeks starting almost immediately.'

'I do?'

'I'm telling you that you have to take time off, and you're upset?'

'No, sorry.'

'Good, then I'll pencil you in to be off for two weeks, starting Monday next, right?'

'Oh.' Was it fate? Two whole weeks, in another place, a place where no one knew her? That was exactly the medicine that Shirley had prescribed, except for the size of the dose.

Constance picked up the phone and got an outside line. Forty minutes later, she was booked for two weeks at Gran Playa Aphrodite, an all-inclusive, adults-only resort on the north coast of the Dominican Republic. Now she'd have to do some serious shopping. The one swimsuit she owned had a Peter Pan collar, legs and sleeves. It had just been worn for her 'girls only' segregated swimming lessons. Somehow, she didn't think it'd go down so well in the Caribbean, particularly the pattern of yellow duckies.

Chapter Six

When she alighted from her plane it was dark out. The air was as warm as fresh-squeezed milk. The airport was all grass huts and exotic plants, though the huts had been built out of two-foot-thick timbers that were held together by massive steel bolts.

A trio of pretty girls in flowery dresses greeted the passengers with weary '*Ola*'s and a few desultory dance steps. Well, it *was* eleven at night. There'd been headwinds. They were three hours late. The travellers were whisked through customs and into an open area that had buses parked around its perimeter. Hers was clearly labelled. Just twenty minutes after she'd landed, her bus was tunnelling its way between dark green walls of dense foliage. Constance caught glimpses of distant gas stations and fizzing neon signs but for most of the following hour it was just gigantic leaves brushing at the sides and roof of the bus and sharp turns taken too quickly. Then there was an open gateway that would have accommodated

King Kong, and she was there, at the resort, in the place where she'd be free to explore her own immodesty to her heart's content – but not until after a good night's sleep and a long hot shower.

Once she'd booked in, a good-looking man in black short-shorts and a white T-shirt loaded her luggage onto a golf cart and whisked her along a many-curved driveway to her room on the ground floor of a three-storey modern pink-brick building. Constance tried to listen while he explained the mysteries of the air conditioning and so on to her. By the time he was done, she only had the energy to wash quickly and crawl into bed stark naked, for just the second time in her young life.

Constance was woken by happy squeals and splashes. The dappling of light on her ceiling told her there was brilliant sunshine and moving waves just a few feet beyond her gauze-draped French windows.

It was all waiting for her – people with admiring lascivious eyes – perhaps romance – certainly some sort of adventure.

And she was terrified.

Of course, she didn't *have* to expose herself to risk and potentially to shame. The room had everything: a lovely onyx-tiled bathroom, a king-sized bed (for one?), a minibar and room service. There were likely to be some English-language programmes available on the 50-inch flat-screen TV. If she decided to chicken out, she could stay in her room for her two weeks, resting, just being idle. If courage came to her tomorrow, she could venture out then. If she never summoned the nerve, well, no one would know or care that she'd been a coward. She could lie to Shirley, make up tales of all sorts of wild adventures.

And her mother would have won. That was a sickening thought.

One step at a time, she told herself. Just do what comes naturally first, then see where that leads. Don't think ahead. Don't look behind. It was still morning, just. In the morning, she always got up and had a shower. So that's where she'd start.

Constance hadn't noticed it the night before but the air in the bathroom was scented. The shower itself was adjustable in a dozen different ways. She luxuriated, which isn't the same as procrastinating. When she washed her intimate parts, Constance made a conscious effort not to avert her eyes.

As she stepped out, she remembered that the resort had hung a fluffy white robe on the bathroom door for her, on the outside. She could always wrap herself in a bath towel, but the robe was only a door away. She opened it.

'So sorry, Miss. Housekeeping. You didn't hear me?'

Constance reached to snatch the robe from its hook but the maid beat her to it and held it out to help her on with. Hoping that her flush from the hot water concealed her blushes, Constance braced herself and fumbled for the sleeves. There was no way for the girl to know that this was the first time since her adolescence that another human being had seen her stark naked.

'Thank you!'

'You very pretty.' There was admiration in the young woman's eyes, perhaps more.

'Thanks for that, as well. You're very – kind.' She couldn't very well return the compliment. The girl was quite plain and very thin. She had virtually no bust, but her nipples were very prominent under her clinging white T-shirt. Perhaps Constance should compliment her on them? She had to suppress a giggle at her own thought.

'Anything you need, Miss?'

'No, thank you. I'm Connie. You?'

'Maria.'

'Thank you, Maria.'

'See?' Maria pointed to a heart-shaped do-not-disturb sign lying on the credenza. 'For when ...'

'Thank you.'

'No problem, Miss Connie.'

'Just Connie.'

Constance's tummy rumbled, making her decision about what to do next for her.

For her first foray into the tropical world, Constance chose a beige playsuit. The fitted top had cap-sleeves and came down to about three inches below her bust. The shorts had four-inch legs and rose to a bare inch above her navel. She'd be exposing five or so daring inches of her bare midriff. Might as well jump right in!

There was a 'train station' grass hut about fifty feet from her building's front door. There was a train already waiting. It consisted of an oversized golf-cart and a string of half a dozen two- and four-seater carriages with open sides and a brilliant yellow canvas roof.

The uniformed girl driver greeted Connie with '*Ola*' and pulled away as soon as she was on board. Connie was the only passenger apart from a couple in the last carriage who were far too wrapped up in each other's limbs to be aware that Connie had got on. Even from the far end of the train, she could hear the noises their voracious mouths were making. She focused on the scenery ahead but that didn't block out the wet sounds. Connie squirmed, not quite sure of how she felt about the public display of sexuality.

The buffet building had windows that were three floors high. A dark Hispanic man was replacing a display menu. A sign announced, 'Cover-up Zone'.

Oh hell! Was she underdressed?

Connie asked the man, 'Excuse me?' She made a gesture at her own outfit. 'Am I covered up enough?'

A slow grin spread across his face. 'No problem there, Miss. You plenty covered.'

That was a relief. She went into the dim room and was led to a table for two near the perimeter of the room, facing inwards. There was only a scattering of late breakfasters or early lunch patrons. Although the hot breakfast bar looked as if it was in the process of closing down, a cheerful server helped her heap a plate with scrambled eggs, bacon, sausages and home fries, plus a toasted bagel with butter and raspberry jam on the side. Constance was hungry.

She was halfway through her feast when a woman passed her on the way to the dessert station. The newcomer's raffia wedges clattered on the tile floor. Constance looked up. The woman's top was a poncho-style square of marmalade-coloured gauze. From the back, it was hard to see if she wore anything else. If she had the bottom half of a swimsuit on, there had to be very little of it. Constance could see every twitch of the woman's lean hips through it. Fascinated, she watched as the woman served herself and turned back. Yes, there was a minute triangle of orange fabric covering her pubic mound. No, she had no bra on. The brown discs of her large nipples were plain to see.

The woman twinkled her fingertips at Constance and mouthed, '*Ola*!'

Constance swallowed before returning the greeting.

A movement off to her left caught Connie's eye. A woman, half of a couple, had moved her leg and her skirt had parted up a slit that reached as far as her waist.

And this was a Cover-up Zone? It was very – confusing. The full implications of 'adults-only resort' crashed into Connie's mind. It certainly didn't just mean 'no children'. She'd expected to come to a resort filled with honey-mooners, retired couples and young singles, innocently or romantically disporting themselves in the sun and sea. She'd thought that her two-piece midriff-baring outfits and what she'd considered outrageously short skirts could make her the centre of attraction. If she met the right man, or even men, she'd been prepared to go beyond flirtation, perhaps. Whatever, she had anticipated being among the least modest of the vacationers …

Instead, it seemed that she'd landed herself in some sort of Sodom.

Was she sure? Well, now that the scales had fallen from her eyes, she'd soon be able to tell.

The train was idling outside. Constance said, '*Ola*' and hopped on. The motor's hum deepened and they were away. There were people waiting outside the small casino, the women dressed in everything from beachwear to tropical styled cocktail dresses but nothing actually shocking.

But the players on the tennis courts were topless, both the men and the women. A redhead stopped a serve with her left breast. Her giggling companions, of both sexes, vied to be the ones to kiss her hurt better. Hm.

The train got to the beach. Connie alighted. The snack

bar, about 5,000 square thatched-roof feet of it, had the cover-up sign but half the women inside were topless. Apparently the rules slackened closer to the waves.

The beach was dotted with small tables, umbrellas and loungers, all facing the ocean. Next to the boardwalk there was a row of showers with frosted glass walls and doors. There were bins for used towels and racks for fresh ones. The Aphrodite couldn't be faulted for the way it catered to its guests.

Connie trudged through sand as fine and white as sugar. She glanced down at the lounger she passed. Oh! The man sprawled asleep in it had a crumpled newspaper draped across his hairy chest but he was bare from his navel down, very bare and very large, curled like a gigantic snail out of its shell.

Connie focused straight ahead. Volleyball. Nude volley-ball. The women bounced and jiggled. The men swayed like rope pendulums. Well, that settled that. Sodom it was! She'd come here intending to shock the other vacationers but it was she who was being scandalised. What next? As she made her way back towards the station, Connie considered her options. She could retreat. That would mean hiding in her room. Or she could just hang out, keeping herself to herself. In the clothing she had with her, she'd be invisible anyway. She could do her best with her wardrobe. Going topless wouldn't be so hard, not when most of the other women were also showing off their boobs, as Jeff called them. That way, she might just be able to blend in.

That was funny. She'd have to show her boobs off so as *not* to be noticed.

But blending in wasn't what she'd come for. She was there to be daring – the cynosure of all eyes. The third alternative would be to find some way to stand out from all the other women and become the Queen of Gomorrah.

But how?

Chapter Seven

'I want to see the sexiest outfits that you have in stock, please,' Constance blurted.

An exotic-looking girl stepped from behind the counter and grinned. 'Right on, sister! Sounds like fun.' Her hair was blue-black, obviously dyed. Her features were oriental, Chinese or Korean, Constance thought, but she had enormous luminous eyes and a red dot painted in the middle of her forehead. More, she was wearing a glittering metallic green and gold sari, but a very short one – just above mid-thigh – and four-inch heels. Just to complete Connie's confusion, her accent was flat New York with no affect – the vocal equivalent of dead-pan.

'You wanna stand out in the crowd, right? I can dig it.'

'Can you help me?'

'You see the problem there, right?'

'Problem?'

'You're cute, very cute, and you've got yourself a killer little bod there. Anywhere else all you'd need do is flash some skin to get mobbed by suitors of a variety of sexual persuasions. Here, though, the main competition is a lot of pretty girls and handsome women. Their outfits range from tiny to nil. You might get noticed if you dressed up like a Las Vegas showgirl and hired your own band, but that'd seem a bit needy, doncha think? And wearing all those feathers would be a bit of a drag, if you'll forgive the pun.'

Constance grinned agreement.

The girl continued, 'You been down to the beach yet?'

'Yes.'

'Lots of naked girls and women there?'

'Yes.'

'Were they being stared at?'

'Not particularly.'

'Y'know why?'

'Why?'

'Being nude is like "all done". They've arrived where they were going. After a girl's naked, there's nothing more to look forward to. Strippers undress on stage. They don't come out already bare, right? It's the peeling that's sexy.'

'You think I should put on a strip-show?'

'Nah. That'd be over sooner or later. What you want is to *look* like you're doing a strip, or you're just about to.'

'Tease them?'

'Exactly.'

'I still don't get it.'

'You wanted to know what the sexiest thing I got for sale is?'

'Yes.'

'It's this.' She reached down a glass vial full of a clear liquid.

'Spray-on paint?'

'No. It's called "Strip-Tack". Exotic dancers use it.' She picked up a length of fabric that looked as if it'd been sewn out of pale green fog. 'Watch.' Deft fingers dabbed a tiny droplet onto one corner of the scarf. She touched that corner to her wrist and let go. The scarf hung. 'Pull it off.'

Constance tugged. The fabric pulled on the girl's skin but it didn't come free.

'Now peel it.'

Constance got a nail under a corner and peeled the fabric away easily. 'I see the possibilities!'

'Good for you! I'm Tina, by the way.'

'Constance – Connie.'

'So you see the possibilities, huh, Connie? Now try this on.' She took a little black dress from a rack. 'That should fit you.'

There was a changing room, which, considering how casual everyone was about nudity, seemed quite strange, but Connie used it. From the waist down the dress was flouncy layers of fine black net. Above the waist, it had no back or sides at all, just a black satin 'M' that had points that reached just high enough to barely cover Connie's nipples. It was held up by a spaghetti strap that looped behind her neck. From the front it was provocative. From the side it was very close to indecent – sexier, Connie realised, than topless would have been.

'You like the look?' Tina asked her.

'Daring.'

'That's what you wanted, right. Now try it like this.'

The spaghetti strap was fastened to the bodice by a pair of tiny hooks and fabric loops. Tina inserted two fingers between the dress and Connie's left nipple.

Connie shivered at the contact but she couldn't very well reject her new friend's help, could she? Anyway, she wasn't sure that she wanted to.

A dab and a press on each nipple, and the bodice stayed up even after the strap had been removed.

'Move around in it,' Tina suggested. 'See how secure it is.'

'Won't it ruin the dress?' Connie asked. She shrugged and twirled but the fabric stayed firmly in place.

'It's water-soluble.'

'So not for swimming.'

'Never say never.'

'You're bad.'

'You too.' Tina smiled a wicked smile. 'Imagine, you at a party in that dress? Who is everyone going to be watching?' In affected accents, she drawled,

'"How *does* she keep it on, my dear?" "It's positively *indecent*." "By Jove, old chap, that gal's about to spill her pretty little titties."'

Connie giggled.

Tina added, 'You'd be a wardrobe malfunction waiting to happen, or look like one. You know how much attention those get.'

Connie told her, 'You're a genius, Tina.'

'True.' Tina reached two fingers into each side of Connie's dress, where the fabric was stuck to her nipples, and worked it loose, taking what seemed to Connie an awfully long time about it.

Connie was about to comment, though she wasn't sure what to say, when Tina's lips were on hers and Tina's tongue was squirming into Connie's mouth. Stunned, Connie froze but didn't respond. It wasn't at all like when a boy kissed her for the first time. Then, she'd always known how she was going to react, in advance.

Tina pulled back. 'Sorry! I guess I misread the signals.'

'No, it's OK, Tina. It's just that I've never been kissed by a girl before.'

'Really? How'd you like it?'

'I'm not sure.'

'Fair enough. Think about it some, huh?'

'I will, I promise.'

'And if you ever want to try again …?'

'I'll be sure to let you know.'

'Right.' Tina became all business. 'How many outfits are you going to need, Connie?'

'Oh – lots.'

'That'll be expensive.'

'No problem, within reason. I'll look on it as an investment.'

Tina took a pair of boy-cut shorts from a drawer. 'How about these? What I'd do to them for you would be ...'

Giggling like schoolgirl conspirators, the two young women sorted through at least a week's worth of garments for Tina to 'convert', and a few accessories. She promised to have them all ready for the following morning. To tide Connie over, Tina found her a minute yellow bikini that she called a 'teardrop' because each of the three patches of fabric connected by thin tapes was the shape of a teardrop – and not a lot bigger. To cover it up she found a matching cropped bolero jacket and a wrap-over skirt that overlapped itself by no more than three inches.

Connie grinned. When she'd arrived at the Dominican Republic, less than a day ago, she'd have considered this skimpy little outfit the ultimate in daring. Now she was looking on it as her base-line, her most conservative set, to fill in while the really hot stuff was being prepared for her.

'You've got time to start on your tan before supper,' Tina suggested. 'Try the Mo-Mo – Japanese. The food is good and so is the show. It's also a good place to meet people.'

'Thanks, for the advice and for everything.'

Connie left, heading for the pool outside her building, and to expose herself more than she'd ever exposed herself before, but only half as much as she planned to expose herself tomorrow.

Wasn't there a song something like that?

Chapter Eight

Almost all of the loungers around the gigantic hexagonal pool were occupied. One, directly outside the French doors to Connie's room, next to a sunbathing older couple, mid-forties perhaps, was conveniently vacant. Connie put her hands on her towelling robe's self-belt. She posed as she'd imagined she would ever since she'd started planning this vacation. No one took any notice so she had to visualise an expectant audience. She gave a silent '*voila*' and tossed her robe aside.

The woman raised her sunglasses and said, 'Nice.'

Connie looked down into amused amber eyes, partially hooded by heavily gilded lids. 'Oh! Your sunglasses ... I didn't realise I was being looked at.'

'I second that,' the man said. 'The "nice", I mean. I'll even add a "very".'

Blushing but pleased, Connie said, 'Thank you.' She looked him up and down. Although he wasn't young, the man had a deeply tanned, lean, triangular body. His sunglasses were mirrors. His hair was crisp and black, with a delicate frosting. As older men went, he'd most certainly qualify as a partner for a holiday romance, or would have done if he hadn't been with the woman.

His companion was as lean as he was but certainly feminine. Even if her bare breasts were 'A' cup at the best, they were firm and self-supported, with nipples the size and colour of hazel nuts. The bikini bottom that she wore wasn't quite as skimpy as Connie's, but was close.

She tossed her pixie-cut auburn hair and introduced them. 'I'm Selena. He's Rupert.' She had a slight European accent that Connie couldn't identify.

'I'm Connie.' She nodded at them in turn. 'Selena. Rupert.'

'Nice to meet you, Connie,' he said. He sounded English. 'Selena, I'm off to fetch a drink. Something for you ladies? One of those pineapple and melon things for you, lovey?'

'Please.'

Connie said, 'That sounds nice, if it isn't too much trouble.'

Two strides and a long flat dive took him into the pool. Selena patted the lounger beside her. Connie sat.

'Honeymoon?' Selena asked.

'No.'

'Boyfriend? Girlfriend?'

'On my own,' Connie confessed.

'Having a good time?'

'I intend to. I only arrived last night.'

'Hell-bent on raising a little hell, right?'

Connie shrugged carefully, unsure how secure her bra was.

'There are plenty of attractive men here,' Selena continued. 'One big advantage to the local dress code – you get an advance view of the goodies – saves disappointments.'

'I imagine most of the men here are taken,' Connie said.

'Well, there's "taken" and then there's "taken", if you see what I mean.'

Connie wasn't sure that she did. Was this woman offering her the use of her husband or boyfriend or whatever Rupert was to her?

'This is a tops-optional area,' Selena suggested with a nod towards Connie's breasts.

'It's my first real day here. I'm still adjusting to the local – culture.'

'I quite understand.' She raised an eyebrow. 'I'll try to be patient.'

Connie covered her confusion by giggling.

'I'm *bad*,' Selena admitted. 'I haven't offended you, I hope?'

'No, not at all.'

'I wouldn't want to scare you away. Rupert would never forgive me.'

Connie moved to the vacant lounger and stretched out. Being perched on the edge of Selena's seat was beginning to feel awkward. The woman was definitely flirting with her, as had Tina, in the boutique. Was it her? Did she give off lesbian vibes, or something? But she wasn't a lesbian, so what did that mean? It was all so confusing.

Or could she be gay and not know it?

Rupert returned with their drinks. Connie's was sweet but not too sweet. As she swallowed, a delightful warmth spread through her body. 'What's in this?' she asked.

'Pineapple juice, melon juice, Midori and rum. How do you like it?'

'I like it.' She took another swallow.

'Take your time,' Selena warned. 'That's 150 proof rum, and they don't skimp.'

'Thanks for the warning.'

'We wouldn't want anyone taking unfair advantage of you while you're tipsy,' Rupert said.

Selena added, 'Unless it's us.'

Connie felt herself turning crimson. Wherever this was going, it was moving too fast. A girl has to take her time deciding which sins she's going to embrace, doesn't she? To buy herself some, she put her sunglasses on and settled back as if to nap, though she remembered to turn her knees to the side and cross her ankles, as Shirley had taught her.

Then someone was touching her arm. She *had* dozed off. It had to be the rum.

'Sorry,' Selena said. 'I hate to spoil your sleep but this is your first day here. Did you put plenty of sun block on? A burn can spoil a holiday big time.'

'Sun block? Oh! I didn't think. I must get some.'

'You're turning pink already. You need it *now*. Here.' She passed Connie a very expensive looking spray bottle.

Connie spritzed into her right hand and smoothed the cream over her shoulder as economically as she could. It wouldn't do to take advantage of a stranger's generosity.

Selena said, 'No, no, dear girl. Be lavish! Here, turn over and I'll do your back for you.'

Connie obeyed. The spray was chilly enough to make her shiver but her skin soon warmed under Selena's rotating palms. Connie concentrated on the sensations. Selena's touch was sure and efficient. It certainly didn't feel as if the woman was using the cream as an excuse for a crafty fondle, not even when she applied her fingers to the curves of Connie's bottom and the backs of her thighs.

When Selena tapped her shoulder and said, 'Over,' Connie didn't hesitate.

Once more, Selena's touch was impersonal. Connie's breasts were jiggled a bit, but that was inevitable. Her nipples didn't slip out from beneath their shielding scraps of fabric even though they threatened to. Was Connie disappointed that they hadn't?

She let her head loll to the side so that she could see Rupert through slitted eyes. He was watching the progress of Selena's hands intently, with no pretence at indifference. If he'd been wearing trunks instead of shorts she was sure they would have betrayed his approval. That was more like it. She'd come here to be looked at. At last, someone was paying her the attention she deserved – and craved. In automatic response, her back arched. If she'd been a cat, she'd have purred.

Selena's hands stilled. 'Oh dear!'

'What is it?' Connie asked.

'Did no one tell you about the bare-hair rule?'

'What?'

'If skin is bare, it mustn't have hair. You – your lower tummy – your pubes – there's a little ...'

'Fuzz?'

'It's very fine,' Selena reassured her, 'and very pale, but still ...'

'I should have it trimmed, do you think?'

'More than "trimmed", I'd say. If that bikini is a fair sample of the sort of things that you plan to wear, you are going to need a total wax job. And you'll need it for the beach, anyway.'

'Damn!' Connie said. 'My other swimsuit, the one I came here with, covered me – down there. I bought this one today.'

'There's nothing for it, Connie. Do you have anything planned for tomorrow morning after breakfast?'

'No, nothing special.'

'Good.' Selena took a cell from her purse and hit a number. Her conversation with whoever she'd called was animated and friendly, and in Spanish, so Connie had no idea what was being said. When Selena hung up, she told Connie, 'I already had an appointment at the Spa, at ten-thirty. They've managed to squeeze you in as well. Is that OK?'

'Thank you very much! Of course it'll be OK. I …' Her voice dried up as the implications sank in. She was going to be waxed, down there! It'd be a woman doing it, she was sure, but even so … She wanted it so much, but she was scared of it. Was that crazy?

'I'll hold your hand,' Selena promised.

Rupert opened his mouth as if to say something but evidently changed his mind. He tapped his paper-thin gold watch. 'Time, lovey!'

'Oh yes. Sorry, Connie, but we have some people we promised to see. Tomorrow, ten-thirty?'

'I'll be there, and thanks again.'

'Think nothing of it.'

They departed, leaving Connie with a cold spot in her tummy. She'd only just met them but they were the closest things she had to friends on the Island, not counting Tina, who was on the staff so didn't count in the same way. Now she was alone again and suddenly lonely, almost adrift. She'd thought that what she mentally referred to as 'an adventure' with the couple had been in the offing. It might still be, but not quite yet. She felt that she was ready to take chances but the chances had just walked away. Tomorrow, she'd grasp every opportunity, no reservations. That was a firm promise!

Connie sunbathed for another half hour before going back to her room. She took a shower, paying extra attention to her pubic area. After all, it was going to be on display in the morning. She had no choice but to put the same bikini back on, but covered by her bolero jacket and mini-skirt. All the clothes she'd packed had turned out to be too conservative to wear. When she left the Island, she'd leave them for her maid, Maria. The travel agent had told her that the Dominicans valued gifts of clothing, perfume and suchlike more than cash. Manufactured goods were in short supply on the Island.

At the Mo-Mo Japanese restaurant, the servers looked like the chorus line for a raunchy version of *The Mikado*. The women were in full geisha makeup and kimonos, but the kimonos were mid-thigh, showing stocking tops, and their shoes had stiletto heels. The men wore baggy black pants and little sleeveless jackets that left their muscular chests and arms bare. In the background, scaled-down Kodo drums were being played by two men and a woman in abbreviated leotards.

Connie was shown to a circular table that ringed a sunken cooking area. She was given the last of six seats. The fifty-plus woman to her left, in an off-the-shoulder peasant blouse from which her ample breasts spilled, introduced herself as Blodwin before turning back to the young Latino on her other side.

The man on Connie's right, blond-haired, chiselled, in a Langouste shirt, Bermuda shorts and Birkenstocks, told her that he was 'Sten – architect'.

She responded with 'Connie – actuary'.

He seemed to like that.

A gong sounded. Their chef, in his high hat and checked pants but with his muscular and clean-shaven chest bare, gave a rotating bow, North, West, South and East. If it hadn't been for his exposed physique, Connie might have been confused about his gender. He was incredibly pretty and wore a touch of eye-liner.

He produced a wrapped rolled-up steak and spread it onto his hot plate, where it sizzled immediately, all two square feet of it. The chef scooped up four pots of spices and herbs to juggle above the meat with one hand while his other snatched them from the air one at a time to sprinkle on the steak. Pots set aside, he took a pair of vicious-looking cleavers and stroked them blade-on-blade until the metal sang. After three preliminary tosses and catches, his hands blurred above the meat. In a matter of a minute or less, the beef had been Julienned into thin slices of almost identical bite-sized dimensions. A wave of his left-hand cleaver spread the meat again, while his right divided it into six equal portions. Square stainless-steel plates appeared. The cleavers scooped and flipped, creating six jack-straw piles, one on each plate. A flourish of sour cream and a single perfect cherry tomato topped each pile before it was dusted with a pale green herb and was presented to the diners.

Before they'd finished applauding, the chef was slivering scallops and shucking oysters.

Connie had used chopsticks before but didn't feel adept, so she took up the fork the restaurant provided. Sten leaned over and with his right hand pointed to the row of jars that sat in front of Connie's plate. His left hand, naturally, landed gently on her bare knee.

'Wasabi,' he told her. 'Very hot. Be careful. This is sesame oil. Soy sauce. Furikake, for fish only. Ponzu.'

'Thank you, Sten.'

His fingers moved an inch higher up her thigh.

The beef disintegrated on her tongue. Connie experimented with the sauces, avoiding the Furikake, so as not to seem gauche. The wasabi was hot, as she'd been warned, but following it with a little sour cream put the excess fire out.

Geishas served sake and Kirin beer. Sten slowly stroked higher. He was about her age, good-looking, a professional and Scandinavian. That's the sort of combination a girl of her age, on vacation alone, dreamed about, right?

But he'd been so damned condescending about the condiments. For all he knew, she ate Japanese cuisine every day. And now his fingertips were under the hem of her skirt, nearing the areas that should be bare, according to Selena, but still bore hair.

Was it that, or had she somehow, in an oblique sort of way, promised herself that her first sexual adventure on the Island would be with Selena? Whichever, Connie excused herself and went back to her room where she caught up on two of her favourite sitcoms.

Chapter Nine

Tina delivered Connie's new and enhanced outfits at eight-thirty in the morning. 'I'd stop while you try them out,' she said, 'but I've got to open up. Shame. I'd love to see what you look like in a few of them.'

'You will,' Connie promised. 'Do you ever get a day off?'

'Sunday.'

'Busy next Sunday?'

'No, but you might be. You're going to make a whole lot of new friends real fast in those outfits.'

'I'll reserve Sunday for you, if you'd like us to do something together.'

'I would. Sunday, then.' She pecked Connie's cheek and scurried away.

Connie would have liked to try every last item on but there wasn't time. She dressed in the first one she opened. It was very simple, a plain white loose-fitting poet shirt and a pair of boy-cut shorts. Tina had reduced the front panels of the shirt so that the edges could no longer be made to meet. It barely stretched to cover her nipples. It couldn't be done up but was held in place by dabs of Strip-Tack, leaving Connie with a six-inch wide full-length cleavage. The zipper fly of the shorts had been sewn so that it could only be zipped halfway up, leaving a wide 'v' of the naked skin on her tummy, pointing to, and almost reaching, her pubes. Once more, a couple of dabs secured the fabric to her skin. No matter how Connie stood, it looked as if her shirt was about to flap open to fully expose her breasts and her shorts were on the brink of sliding off her body and dropping to the ground, baring everything else. Clever Tina!

Connie dropped the little bottle into her purse. If she was to get dressed somewhere else, like at the Spa, she'd need it, really need it.

She took a deep breath and headed for the train station.

There was a couple already there, waiting under the palm-frond roof. As she approached, the woman nudged the man and said something. He half turned to look at Connie. His eyes widened. He sucked his gut in and pushed his chest out. Bliss. *This* was what she'd been fantasising about!

Connie arrived at the Spa precisely on time. She liked to be punctual, even in the Caribbean. A pretty little mixed-race girl greeted her by name in broken English and led her to a changing room. There she left her clothes hanging and exited naked under a brief pink satin self-tie wrap and wearing a matching pair of pom-pom mules. Where was Selena?

'There you are!' The woman's voice came from behind her.

Connie turned. Selena was dressed identically to her, except that her wrap was pale blue. She was carrying a couple of opened coconuts adorned with tiny umbrellas and maraschinos on sticks.

'A bracer, or would you rather not? Just in case you need Dutch courage.'

'It's way too early, but yes, I will, thanks.'

Selena led her into a very feminine room that was equipped with a pair of massage tables, a vanity and shelf after shelf of lotions and potions. There was a full-length mirror set into the ceiling above each padded table. She'd be able to watch what they did to her, which was an exciting thought. She'd also be able to see what went on at the other table, Selena's. And Selena would be able to see her. It was the last thought that gave her the strongest tingles.

'Mine's started to grow out,' Selena said.

'How often do you do it?' Connie asked.

'About once a month is what Rupert likes and, as far as I'm concerned, what Rupert likes, Rupert gets.' The elegant woman cast her wrap aside, hopped up onto the table and lay flat on her back.

'That's sweet!'

'He's very good to me, Connie. A man like that is hard to find and well worth taking an extra effort to please, don't you think?'

Connie thought of all the times she'd refused Jeff's modest requests and felt a wave of guilt. 'I couldn't agree more,' she whispered. Inside, she resolved that sooner or later, she'd make it up to Jeff, even if they didn't become a couple again. She owed him that, at least.

And the next step in recreating herself was happening right now. She shrugged out of her wrap just as if baring her body in public was routine for her, and mounted her table.

There she was, in the mirror above her head. And there was Selena, in the next mirror. Connie had the advantage of youth but there was something very sensuous, almost serpentine, about Selena. If Connie had been a third party, asked to choose which of those two naked women she wanted to make love to, it'd have been a hard decision to make.

What was she thinking? She'd only ever kissed one woman before in her entire life, Tina – and now she was having the most depraved thoughts without even shocking herself?

Six pretty young women filed in, carrying large plastic bags. Four set up tables beside Connie and Selena's heads and feet. Two set them up at the ends.

Selena told Connie, 'While we're at it, I thought mani-
pedis would be nice.'

'Lovely!'

'Next time, we could use the sauna and have massages,
if you like.'

Next time? That had to mean that Selena saw their friend-
ship continuing and developing – just so Connie didn't let
her old modest habits get in the way and blow it. Just as
Selena had said about Rupert – 'What he wants, he gets'
– Connie resolved the same about Selena. No matter what.

She found her fingers being inserted into slippery
liquids. Presumably to soak. She'd never been inside
a beauty parlour before, let alone been given the full
decadent treatment.

Delicate little hands took hold of her ankles. A
matching voice asked, 'Please?'

She allowed her feet to be spread and discovered that
the foot of the table was made to divide into a V so that
the attendant could stand almost between her knees.
Connie's calves brushed either side of the woman's warm
hips. The attendant held up a spray can and asked a
question that Connie didn't understand. She looked at
Selena in her mirror.

'It's a mild topical analgesic, optional. Do you want it?'

'Do you use it?'

'Some women quite enjoy the sensation of a waxing,
even if it does hurt a little bit,' Selena answered obliquely.

'Then I won't, thanks.' She smiled and shook her head at the attendant.

The woman smoothed on latex gloves. 'OK. This little bit hot-hot. You ready?'

'Yes.' She looked up at the mirror to watch the woman's deft fingers use a spatula to slather her mound and lower tummy with a pearlescent cream. It was very warm, almost hot, but not unbearable. She glanced to the side. Selena was watching her. They exchanged grins. Partners in decadence.

'Lift, please.'

Connie raised her bottom. The woman slid a foam plastic wedge beneath her, tilting her hips up. One of those could be fun, if she ever got back with Jeff.

Connie closed her eyes to concentrate on the sensations. Her nails were clipped and filed and smoothed. Her cuticles were tended to. Creams were massaged into her fingers and toes. When it seemed that her right hand was done, she peeked and found that Selena was still watching her. Her new friend reached out a hand. Connie took it. It was … companionable, holding hands, naked, while exotic foreigners groomed her so intimately.

It was everything her mother abhorred.

She was naked, with seven naked or half-naked women all looking at her body, one of them from so close to her taboo parts that she had to be able to make out every individual pore. There was touching, and watching. The sheer obscenity of her situation overwhelmed her and excited her. At last, she was truly alive.

The young attendants were chattering and giggling but in Spanish, so Connie couldn't understand more than the odd word, such as *bellísima*. It certainly sounded as if they approved of her.

Connie looked a question at Selena.

'They're admiring your body, Connie. They think that you are beautiful.'

They burst into laughter.

Selena continued, 'They're discussing the things they'd like to do to and with you if one of them had you on her own.'

'Really?'

'Really.'

'Um ... Do? Such as? Well, I can't help be curious.'

'Of course not, but the sort of thing they suggest, I think I should know you better before I tell you.'

The girl between Selena's legs was compressing and relaxing a palm on her mound. It felt as if lust was being pumped into her pubes. Connie concentrated on that, mainly because it was making it hard for her to think straight. With her newly manicured right hand she reached for her coconut and took another suck.

A triangle of white wide-mesh cloth was spread over Connie's pubes and tucked in beneath her, all the way up between the cheeks of her bottom. Her attendant massaged her through the fabric with a touch that was pleasant, to say the very least. More of the pearly wax was spread on top and then sprayed from a pump-bottle.

'That solution hardens the wax,' Selena explained. 'You'll have a rigid shell there in a few moments, just like a tortoise.' She picked up her drink and saluted Connie. 'Here's to the hairless, the smooth and the bold. When pussies are bald, no man can be cold.'

Connie spluttered her drink. A server handed her a tissue for her nose.

Selena said, 'Sorry.'

'You're so funny.'

Selena grinned. 'I think it's time, Connie.'

'Time for what?' Then she felt fingertips pry under the edges of the wax shell that encased her pubes. 'Oh.'

The server ripped.

'Oh, er, um, oh!'

'You OK?' Selena asked.

'I'm good,' Connie lied. Or was it a lie? It had been painful, like a flash of fire, but just for a split second and not *that* painful. Now the entire area was glowing in a way that was rather nice. And so sensitive, like Jeff's pumiced fingertips had felt to him, perhaps.

The girl stroked gently across Connie's mound. The sensation was exquisite.

Selena told her, 'Now you get your reward.'

'What's that?'

'You'll see. Just lie back and enjoy. That's what I'm going to do.'

Connie glanced down her body to see what was going on. The young woman stationed between her knees was setting up a magnifying glass on a stand.

'They're meticulous,' Selena explained.

'Oh.'

The attendant bent close to the magnifying glass, holding a pair of fine tweezers.

'When she's done with you, there won't be a single hair down there, not one.'

It was strange, lying there having her private parts prodded and poked and inspected and occasionally gently plucked. The touches were impersonal but that didn't make them less pleasant; in fact, in a perverse way, it added to the pleasure. Connie looked up to watch what was being done to Selena. The older woman looked a lot different, down there. Whereas Connie had a tight little slit, very smooth and almost featureless, Selena's sex was convoluted, with protruding wrinkled lips. It seemed that women came in a wide variety of formations. Which would a man prefer, simple and pure or complex and sort of obscene?

It'd be interesting to get a closer look at Selena's anatomy. And how about Tina? Would she be different again down there? And Shirley? What a world it was, with so many interesting possibilities waiting for her to explore. Even here, in this one small room, there were eight pussies, each with its own very individual quirks.

'Next it's a mild antiseptic,' Selena explained, 'followed by a moisturising cream, and then we're done.' She paused. 'Connie, don't be embarrassed if you find yourself reacting, OK?'

'Reacting?'

'You'll see.'

The compressing and relaxing on her mound started again but with the compressions becoming stronger with each squeeze, and gradually accelerating in pace. Connie checked Selena's mirror. The older woman was enjoying the same intimate massage. Selena's face was a total blank, as if she'd withdrawn into herself to focus entirely on the sensations.

While one of the young woman's hands continued to pump Connie's mound, the latex-sheathed fingers of the other took gentle hold on the lips of her sex and manipulated them subtly. Beside Connie, Selena sighed.

The lips of Connie's sex were being worked together. Connie could feel them engorging. The tantalising fingers moved a fraction higher. Her clitoris was being gently nipped so that it slid in and out of its sheath, being masturbated.

It felt larger than it ever had before, even when Jeff had performed at his very best. The attendant had taken complete control over Connie's sex and sexuality. She was totally helpless. The closest she could come to thinking was realising that her hand was inside the wrap of the girl beside her to her left, kneading her slender thigh desperately. She didn't even know how it had got there. She pulled her hand away but the girl caught her wrist and pulled it back. 'Is OK,' she said, and bent to plant a delicate kiss on Connie's lips.

The lips of Connie's sex were throbbing and engorging. Inside, she felt hot and slithery and then something – two fingers? – thrust into her. Beside her, Selena was moaning. If it was OK for the elegant and sophisticated older woman to express her arousal so blatantly, then …

The thought was never completed. Connie shivered into a gut-wrenching climax. Perhaps she screamed but that might have been someone else.

When her head cleared Connie turned sideways to look directly into Selena's eyes. 'What,' she asked, 'would be an appropriate tip for these girls?'

Chapter Ten

When you plan to try a new experience and spend a lot of time in the anticipation, it rarely turns out exactly as you expect. Mostly, the real thing falls short of the imagined one. Once in a while, the reality is better than you'd anticipated. Connie wasn't sure how she'd class her vacation so far, on living up to expectations. She'd planned to be the centre of attraction because of how daringly she'd be dressed. That was supposed to lead to her being courted by numerous good-looking men. Then, apart from bathing in masculine admiration, her idea had been to flirt with them all, bed a few of the choicest specimens, and from there she'd expected a full-fledged holiday romance with Prince Charming, just like in the movies but XXX-rated.

It'd gone sideways right from the beginning. She'd been dowdy by comparison with the other women and girls. She'd taken care of that, with a little help from Tina. She'd been surrounded by lovely admirers, as planned, but, apart from Selena, those had all been commercial relationships. And, apart from some mild flirtation with Rupert, who was 'taken', and Sten's aborted pass, she'd had no real contact with a man.

And she needed that. Intimate contact.

She needed it to confirm her own heterosexuality. Until coming to the Dominican Republic, she'd never even thought about Sapphic love. Almost never, anyway. Her mother had never mentioned that topic; probably it was beyond her conception. That'd be why it hadn't been such intensely forbidden fruit as immodesty was. Every day, Connie's insight was growing.

One thing that her new insight was shouting at her – the only way to resolve her present confusion was to get herself a nice man with a good hard cock and do obscene things to him and it until the poor creature screamed for mercy.

Which was another problem. Leaving the Spa, Selena had told her that Rupert would be having a late solo lunch at The Sheik's Palace and he'd be delighted if she joined him, but not to feel pressured. If she had other plans, that was just fine.

Rupert certainly had a cock. It had to be a fully functional and superior model. Selena wasn't the sort of woman who would settle for less.

Which was another problem. Could she betray her new girlfriend with her husband or whatever Rupert was to her? And then she had yet another consideration – she'd already had sex, in a strange sort of way, with Selena. Was that like them cheating on Rupert?

Penetrating insight was all well and good, except when it led to utter confusion. Best play it by ear. And she'd never tried Arabian cuisine – that'd be a new experience, which is what vacations are for.

Another consideration occurred to Connie – if she *did* have sex with Rupert, that'd mean he'd be cheating on Selena. That'd mean he wasn't worthy of her. If Connie broke them up, she'd actually be doing Selena a favour.

Being an actuary by profession had blessed Constance with a keenly analytical mind. A detailed re-examination of all the facts and factors had now led her to see that she should do exactly what she'd wanted to do in the first place, but feel fully justified and guilt-free. Having a good mind can be so comforting.

From the outside, The Sheik's Palace looked like an overgrown but immaculate tent city. She'd kicked her heels off in the open vestibule before she remembered that she didn't know Rupert's last name, to ask for him by. That problem was solved when a slender girl asked her, 'Miss Connie?'

Connie nodded.

'Mr Rupert is in The Caliph's Pavilion. Please to follow me.'

The hostess was dressed as a harem slave in a tiny brocade bra and gauzy pants over a thong. As she walked, her hips swung further to each side than their own width. She made Shirley's wildest hip-movements look demure by comparison.

The air was scented with patchouli. World music played softly in the background.

Connie was led through a zig-zag passageway between taut canvas walls, none of which stood exactly vertical nor met at right angles. It seemed that the fabric dividers separated private eating areas. From time to time Connie heard muted voices, giggles and squeals. Once, the placing of the hidden lights projected a silhouette of a couple onto a canvas-wall screen, her on her knees before him, bottom high, head low. He was grunting urgently. Connie would have liked to pause to watch the shadow show but her hostess was already turning a sixty-degree corner ahead of her.

The Caliph's Pavilion was a wide and deep multi-level bowl, shadowy, thickly carpeted, furnished with divans, plush chairs and personal-sized tables. Some light filtered in from high above. Some was provided by Aladdin-style lamps, not real ones but with flickering electric flames.

As she was led, Connie's eyes adjusted to the dim light. There were couples and groups of three, even four, in various combinations of gender. As far as she could tell, there was no overt sexual activity going on, just a few kisses and restrained caresses being exchanged in the dimness.

Rupert rose to greet her. With his dark tan, his black T-shirt and black denim jeans, he had been almost invisible until his grin flashed. His eyes widened as he took her flirtatious outfit in but he didn't say anything about it. He held her fingers and raised the back of her hand to his lips. 'Did you enjoy your visit to the Spa?' There was a twinkle in his eye.

'Yes, thanks.'

He pulled her chair out. 'It was all that you expected?'

'More,' Connie admitted. She sat. 'Much more.' Just how much did he know about what had gone on?

'My Selena is a fine hostess.'

'She certainly is.' Might as well get it out and in the open. 'Are you two married?'

'Sort of. We're certainly a couple.' He grinned. 'I think you're asking if we are exclusive.'

Connie blushed. 'It's none of my business, of course.'

'Someone's sexual orientation and relationship status are no business of anyone else's, unless that someone else is interested in starting a relationship, or at least an encounter, don't you agree?'

'Yes, but –'

'So I have to assume that you are interested in a relationship with one of us, either Selena or me, or both.'

Connie was speechless. Her face burned.

'Let's not be coy. I feel that the three of us could become friends, close friends.'

Exactly what did he mean by *that*?

'I believe that you young people call it "friends with benefits".'

'Oh.' That she understood.

'Now,' he said, 'with that out of the way, let's enjoy our meal. It's *carte fixe* here, a different selection each day but no choices. I hope you like lamb.'

'Yes, very much,' she lied. She couldn't remember ever eating it. Her origins were in cattle country.

'In order to preserve the Arabian illusion, the drinks are all called "sherbets", but don't let that fool you. They're all champagne cocktails and quite potent.'

Another harem girl delivered a brass tray on a stand with an assortment of small dishes.

'If there's anything you don't recognise, I'll be happy to describe what they are,' Rupert offered.

'Please. Everything.'

'Well, this strange oriental dish is called hard boiled eggs – chicken eggs. The paprika is for the eggs, optional.'

'How exotic!'

'Indeed. Now, this one isn't all that popular in the West, but I recommend it. It's sweetbreads in a tangy lemon sauce. Next we have lamb chops, already boned for us though I wish they wouldn't do that. The green jelly in that bowl is just mint. We use the toasted pita triangles to dip and scoop. Um – red pepper hummus – baba ghanoush – this one here is a date dip. Too sweet for my taste. For dessert, they'll be bringing us figs stuffed with raw cane sugar and baked, served with clotted cream and with some Turkish Delight on the side. How does that all sound?'

'Lovely,' Connie told him, though she had reservations. She looked around her setting.

'No implements,' Rupert told her. 'We eat with our fingers. See – rosewater fingerbowls, all ready and waiting.' To demonstrate, he scooped a piece of very pale meat covered in lemon sauce up with a piece of pita and held it to Connie's lips.

She'd forgotten what it was called but had little choice but to try it. The meat was very sweet and tender – yes – sweetbreads, that was it, whatever it was. Better not ask. To show she was in the spirit, Connie picked a piece of lamb out of the dish and presented it to Rupert with her bare fingers. He took it with barely a touch of his tongue to her finger-tips. A less refined man would likely have made a show of sucking her fingers. But he still hadn't mentioned her outfit.

There was a musical 'ting'. Rupert looked down to the lower level. 'Here comes the floor show.' Connie followed his eyes.

Two women in belly-dance costumes were wending their way towards them. Their outfits were identical, thin mesh bras that their nipples clearly showed through and abbreviated skirts that looked as if made from golden coins. One wore an emerald stone in her navel, the other a ruby. Otherwise, they contrasted. One was slender, showing off abdominal muscles that spoke of ten thousand crunches. The other had to be twice her partner's weight, at least, with rolling voluptuous curves that jiggled with every step that she took.

A few feet from Connie and Rupert, the women paused and posed, cymbal-adorned fingers curled elegantly above their heads. The background music faded out and restarted with a slow drumbeat. The women's cymbals rang. Their hips swayed in unison. The plump one took a step back, yielding the floor. A sinuous ripple ran up the other's abdomen, deepening the indentation between her abdominal muscles in a steady rhythm. She stepped back and the other advanced. Her tummy writhed, not rippling but moving in a progressive jiggle that indicated that, beneath the fleshiness, she was as toned as her partner.

Connie couldn't help but wonder what it was to be like the dancers, making their living by showing off their bodies, letting people admire them. Some people might think that they were being exploited but to Connie it was the other way round. The dancers were exploiting their audiences. They got to be admired and got paid for it. That'd be hard to beat, as a profession.

Connie swallowed the piece of egg that Rupert had presented to her lips and whispered, 'Duelling tummy muscles.'

He responded with 'Abdo, abdo, abdo, abdo men,' showing that he recognised her reference to 'Duelling Banjos'.

That was nice – companionable. It gave them a connection, like married couples develop.

The fleshy dancer's writhing changed to a twitching of her hips to an accelerating beat until her torso became a shivering blur. She paused. The other dancer repeated the action.

Each challenge was met and countered, elegant shrugs, spine-cracking back bends, hip thrusts that were blatant imitations of – no, Connie wouldn't think a euphemism – of fucking.

Finally they paused, brushed their lips together, bowed and advanced on Rupert, pubes thrust forward, hips still trembling. He tucked bills into the tops of their tiny skirts and they left, skipping.

Connie scooped the last trace of caramelised sugar off the plate of figs, sucked it off her finger and washed it down with a swig of lemon 'sherbet'.

Rupert dabbed his mouth with a napkin. 'Did you want anything else or shall we go?' he asked.

'What did you have in mind?'

'You and your body, of course, Connie. I've thought of nothing else since you arrived in that clever little "about to fall off" outfit.'

'Not even when you were watching those sexy dancers?'

'Dancers? Oh, them. I wasn't watching them. I was looking at you and at the way you were watching them.'

Connie asked, 'Your place or mine?'

He stood and pulled her to her feet. 'Mine, eventually, but before we go ...' Rupert dipped two fingers into a fingerbowl. Looking into her eyes, not at what he was doing, he wet her shirt immediately over her left nipple.

Connie shivered.

'Water-soluble adhesive, right?' he asked.

Connie squeezed out a husky 'Yes'.

Rupert took her by her right hand and pulled her after him through the restaurant and out into the open air with the left side of her shirt flapping behind her and the tropical sun kissing her naked left breast.

Chapter Eleven

No sooner had Connie stepped into her sandals than Rupert broke into a run for the waiting train. She had no choice but to do likewise, with half of her shirt streaming out behind her. He jumped aboard, pulled her up onto the platform and turned her to face outwards at the world. His left hand closed over her left hand, clamping it to a vertical rail. His right hand captured her right hand, against the other rail.

'Aren't we going to sit down?' Connie asked.

'No.'

'What are you doing?'

'Showing my beautiful companion's body off to the entire population of the Dominican Republic, plus any spy satellites that happen to be passing overhead.'

'Oh. What about Haiti?'

'It wouldn't be fair to tease them.'

The train pulled away. There was only a slight onshore breeze but the train headed straight into it, adding ten miles an hour. Connie's shirt fluttered, showing and then concealing her left breast. People they passed nudged each other and grinned and looked after her.

Rupert whispered into Connie's ear, 'Of all the breasts that are being displayed at Gran Playa Aphrodite today, your left one is getting more attention than any other pair and will be the best remembered. Sometimes one is more alluring than two.'

There had to be something clever for her to say but all the eyes that turned her way and dwelt on her left breast were getting to her. Lust-fogged. That was what she was. It was a state of mind she couldn't remember experiencing before. Still, she'd never before been this lusty in a situation where thought was called for.

A topless tennis match paused as they passed. She'd watched the same players yesterday. Now it was they who were staring at her, though she was showing less than either of the girl players. That was exhilarating.

The breeze insinuated airy caresses into the half-open fly of her shorts, sending fluttery thrills into her sex. Connie leaned her head back onto Rupert's so solid shoulder. She arched, lifting her bottom up against him, feeling for some sign of his erection. Ah! It wasn't upright, yet, but it was thick and slanted off to his left. Connie twitched at it, subtly masturbating him with her bum's left cheek.

'Harlot!' he told her.

'Yes,' she agreed. 'And I'm horny. When are you going to do something about that?'

'Enjoy the ride.'

'This one, or the next?'

'Both. They're all looking at you, you know, Connie. All the men and half the women are jealous that it's me who is holding you captive, not them.'

The train pulled away from the gigantic beach snack bar to retrace its meandering route.

Connie said, 'Back at you, Rupert.'

'Thanks, but that isn't so. It's you they are watching. You're in white and in the sunshine. I'm behind you, in the shade, dressed in black. I'm virtually invisible, just part of the background – *your* background.'

'Doesn't it make you jealous that I'm the one getting all the attention?'

'Not in the least. I've arranged it to be so, haven't I? Besides, we're a good match. I like to watch. You like to be looked at. I'm a voyeur and you are an exhibitionist. We fit, just like sadist and masochist, or dominant and submissive.'

'Yin and yang,' Connie mused.

'My Selena swings both ways,' he told her.

The mention of his lovely companion cooled Connie a little. 'You mean she's bisexual?'

'She is, but no. I meant that she's both an exhibitionist and a voyeur. Give her a mirror and a vibrator and she can amuse herself for endless hours, watching herself watching herself.'

Connie giggled. 'Cheap date!'

'Cheap date,' Rupert agreed. 'Fun, though, for a voyeur like me.'

Connie'd had enough of this talk about Selena. 'Which building are you in?'

The train slowed to a halt.

'This one.'

Connie looked around. There was no sign of any of the three-floor pastel brick buildings that housed the suites, just a high white adobe wall with a gated archway.

'We have a villa,' Rupert explained.

'A villa? I didn't see any of those mentioned in the brochure.'

'No, they aren't for vacationers. We own it. We have business here so we spend a lot of time in the compound.'

'You own the Gran Playa Aphrodite?' Connie was impressed, perhaps too impressed.

'No – we just own a couple of concessions within the compound.'

'How nice for you!'

Rupert unlocked the gate and led Connie through. Inside was a small garden, or large patio, in Japanese style: a tiny pool, pebbles, rocks, meticulously raked sand, bonsai and the occasional dramatic cactus.

'Lovely!' Connie exclaimed.

'Low maintenance, as well. I'm not a fanatic. Not about looking after gardens.'

She followed him through the back door into an open-plan ground floor: kitchen, living room and dining room, nicely furnished but in a way that betrayed that it wasn't a real home, more of a pied-à-terre.

'Would you like coffee, or tea, or …?' he asked.

'Where's the bedroom, unless you have another preference? A couch, maybe? Anything horizontal.'

'There's a good girl. This way.'

The bedroom was open to the bathroom. Between them, they took up the entire upper floor. There was a mirror for a bedhead, another set in the ceiling above it and several full-length mirrors scattered around. The décor was a mix of art nouveau and art deco, accented by a dozen elegantly flowing nude bronzes, several with lunar themes.

Rupert led Connie to the vanity in the bathroom. He splashed her front with warm water to dissolve the adhesive that kept her looking indecent. As he tugged her shorts down over her shapely bottom, she shed the shirt that had concealed the plump globe of her right breast.

With two kicks that sent her sandals flying, Connie raced for the bed and threw herself onto her back on it. A moment later Rupert was naked and sprawled beside her.

He raised himself up on two arms. 'Let me look at you!'

She posed, hips turned, ankles crossed, back arched up to present her breasts for his inspection.

Felix Baron

'Lovely!'

'Do me, please, Rupert?' she asked.

'So you talk dirty as well, do you? What are you, perfect or something?'

Connie pouted, 'Please? Pretty please?'

He leaned over her and nibbled at her lips with his. That was nice, but they were naked in bed, for goodness' sake, and she, for one, was desperately horny. Connie had never initiated 'tongues' before, but this time she did. As she probed Rupert's mouth, she wriggled closer, trying to worm her way under his body.

He pulled back. 'No time for foreplay, huh? Would you like a quickie for the first time and we'll take it more leisurely next?'

'What do you think, Rupert? Can't you feel my need?' She moved his hand to her mound.

'Is *that* what's dripping out of you, Connie? Very well, a quickie it is!'

He took hold of her hips and raised her as he rolled so that she was suspended above him. A quick twist and he had her facing his feet. Instinctively, Connie folded her legs and put her feet flat on the bed. He lowered her. The knob of his cock butted her slit, parted it and it entered her.

He maybe wasn't quite as big down there as Jeff, but he was substantial enough, and oh so needed!

Connie could see herself in a mirror opposite. How

many women had watched themselves in that mirror while riding Rupert? However many there were, she was going to give the best show of them all, including Selena.

Emulating the belly-dancers, she rippled her abdomen, tightened her tummy muscles to clamp hard, and did half a dozen quick bumps. As she leaned backwards, she could feel the pressure of his cock's head hard against the front of her vagina.

She swung forward and held his knees. In the mirror, her delicate breasts hung from the arc of her body. She bumped again, grinding his glans against the rear wall of her sex.

Jerk forward.

Jerk back.

Jerk left.

Jerk right.

Rotate, slowly grinding, then faster and faster until she was tossing her hair in a stream and churning her insides with his shaft.

'How beautiful you are,' he told her. 'Nice moves, too.'

She bounced and scrunched down to see just how deeply into her body she could impale herself on him.

In the mirror, she was wild-eyed and slack-lipped with lust. Rupert didn't move, which was good. This was *her* show. He was just a prop, like a stripper's pole, contributing by simply being there.

Poor Jeff had never got to see her like this. Come to

that, she'd never seen herself like it before. What she'd missed! If only she'd known that erotic love involved all the senses. Touch was important, for sure, but so were sight and smell and taste and hearing.

'Your cock feels so good inside me,' she told Rupert. She took in a deep open-mouthed breath to suck in the musk-laden air.

Poor Jeff. She'd been so bad to him. What would he think if he could see her now, gyrating naked and wanton? Would he take a seat in that big chair over there, take his lovely cock out and slowly jerk off as he watched her? She'd stare at his long white shaft as he stared back at the sway of her delicious young breasts or at the rabid desire that infused her face or at the undulating curves of her tummy. From that seat, he wouldn't be able to see her back, her bum, but she and Rupert had only just started. Her rear was bound to be turned towards Jeff sooner or later.

Or would he get out of the chair, cock in hand, and walk around the bed, inspecting their bodies and movements?

How would it be between Rupert and Jeff if they ever met? Neither was gay, or even bi, she was sure of that, but how would they feel about sharing her? One fucking her as she sucked the other? Or one entering her from behind as the other fucked her from in front?

It was as if Rupert read her mind. She felt a warm

wet fingertip stroke across the puckered skin of the knot of her bottom. Connie pushed back to encourage him. The fingertip pressed, and plopped inside.

Oh, it was all so fucking obscene! She felt delirious. Her eyes were glazing over. This had to be the ultimate in desire – or it would be if her fantasy had been reality.

Wait a moment. Was there room in her imaginary orgy for Selena to join in? The lovely woman could be a spectator, at least, applauding the skills and beauty of her young protégé, Connie. Applauding by masturbating? What a tribute that would be!

Connie blinked. Could arousal really give you a high, make you delusional? In the chair where she'd imagined Jeff sitting and jerking off ... Her misty eyes cleared a little. It really did look as if someone was sitting there – someone whose hand was very busy between wide-spread naked thighs.

Rupert said, 'Hi, lovey!'

Chapter Twelve

Selena said, '*Ola*, you two! Would you mind not stopping? Just keep doing what you're doing.' Her voice was very breathy. 'I'm getting really close to a rather nice little climax.'

'No problem,' Rupert said. 'Right, Connie?'

She felt his big hand lock in her hair from behind and pull back and down, arcing her body backwards until it was taut and she was looking straight up at their cheek-to-cheek image in the ceiling mirror. Rupert gave a mighty toss of his hips and got his feet flat on the bed so that he was supporting Connie on the wrestler's bridge of his body. He fucked up into her, jolting her, burying his shaft deeper into her body with each powerful stroke.

Connie turned her head to get her tongue into his mouth. She felt Selena get up out of her chair and come over to the bed. A finger touched her groin. Selena's face was close to where Rupert's column was gripped between the bald lips of Connie's pussy.

'Beautiful,' Selena sighed. 'So lovely. Feel what watching you is doing to me, Connie.' She took the girl's hand, held it to her sex, two fingers tucked inside its flaccid lips, and ground down on its palm. 'Oh yes, Connie, like that! Make me come, you fucking gorgeous little b-b-bitch!'

Connie's fingers were suddenly scalding wet. Selena grunted and fell to her knees beside the bed. The knowledge that it was Selena's watching her that had driven the woman into her climax was enough to tip Connie over the edge into her own. She clenched inside. Her toes curled. She sucked on Rupert's mouth and tongue, desperately thirsty for the essence of him.

And Connie came.

The women both lay and panted for a few minutes.

'I should have told you that when I climax I get very wet,' said Selena apologetically.

Connie chuckled. 'It'd have been more of a surprise if it'd been my mouth that you squirted into.' She was amazed at her own boldness. A few short months ago, she'd been a prude, a passionate one, but a prude none the less. Now she was transformed into a blatant sexual show-off who said, without shame, things that would have scandalised her former self.

Selena said, 'Next time you make me come, consider yourself warned, OK?'

'Sure.' Connie thought for a moment. 'You two set

this up, didn't you?' she accused. 'You catching me in bed with Rupert?'

'Of course. You love to be watched, so that's what we arranged for you. Are you upset?'

'That was the *best*. How could I possibly be upset?' She rolled off the bed and crawled over to where Selena lay on her back. 'This is how upset I am.' She kissed the woman, long and slow, not with lust or even love, but with a deeply felt, tender affection, the way she imagined lesbian sisters might kiss.

Now where did that thought come from?

'May I get you ladies something?' Rupert asked.

Rupert! Oh, the poor man. She was so blissed-out with the aftermath of her climax that she was neglecting him. He'd been so good to her, for half the day, not just in bed. With Selena's help, he'd given her such a spectacular and satisfying orgasm, and here she was, on the floor with Selena, leaving him all alone with what had to be a really ferocious erection.

She stood and went to the bed. Yes, there it was, engorged and stiff, just standing there. Connie wrapped her hand around its shaft and gave it a little squeeze. 'Wouldn't you like me to take care of this for you first?'

'No rush.'

Selena explained, 'He's a man, Connie dear, not a boy. He'll get his in due course, don't worry. There are two willing women here, after all. Meanwhile, my Rupert loves to be kept feeling horny.'

'Anticipation is half the pleasure,' Rupert added.

'Well,' Connie assured him, 'whenever you've enjoyed enough of the anticipation half of the pleasure, I'm ready, willing and able to provide the other half.'

'Meanwhile, a glass of wine, perhaps?'

'That would be nice.'

'Burgundy?'

'I'm no connoisseur – of wine.' There was a tiny crystalline bead in the eye of his cock. Connie lapped it up with the tip of her tongue, her eyes on his, promising.

'You're quite the accomplished seductress for a girl your age, Connie,' Selena said.

'Just doin' what comes unnaturally.'

A bedside cabinet turned out to be a wine rack. While Rupert poured, Selena went to the bed and sat hip-to-hip with Connie. 'Sex is great fun for you, isn't it, Connie?'

'It is now. I used to have some inhibitions that spoiled it for me, some. It's certainly fun with you two.'

'You've had man troubles in the past?'

Connie nodded. 'With one particular man.'

'Over him yet?'

'Not quite.'

'Then we shall do our best to take your mind off him – unless you plan to get him back?'

'It's complicated.'

'It always is.'

'I've learned a lot since I came here.'

'That's good.'

'Mainly from you two. You've made me very confident in my ...'

'Powers?'

'I guess. Powers of seduction.'

'Are you planning to use your new abilities to get that man back, once you go home?'

'I could. I know I could, if I wanted and set my mind to it.'

'So?'

'My eyes have been opened. I don't know that I'm ready for monogamy again, not just yet.'

'Love can be special without the sex being exclusive, you know.'

'If both of the couple feel the same way. You two have something really special going for you.'

Rupert sat on the other side of Selena and put his arm around her. 'We haven't patented it. In our opinion, we have the perfect life, but other people can achieve the same if they truly want it. Our work is our play. We do both together. We are partners in everything, joined at the hip, as they say.'

'Your work is your play? What exactly is it that you do, apart from owning franchises?'

Rupert and Selena leaned forward to exchange looks

past Connie. Both shook their heads slightly. Rupert said, 'We'll get into that in due course. Be patient, please.'

Connie said, 'You're very mysterious, you two. What's going on? I feel like I'm being interviewed for a job or something. You looking for an actuary?'

'If we told you, there'd be no mystery. Wait, and enjoy the anticipation, OK?'

Connie drained her glass. 'I'll be patient,' she promised. 'Meanwhile, there are three rather attractive naked bodies here. What shall we do with them?'

Selena said, 'As you're the guest, your choice, Connie.'

'So I get to pick who does what to who?'

'Exactly,' Rupert said.

Connie considered that. Directing would be fun, wouldn't it, but if she made the wrong choices it could ruin everything. Everyone who is sane has sexual limits. It was unlikely this kinky couple had any that she didn't share but, even so, what she chose could tell them a lot about her. It was like selecting forks at a banquet, or being asked to decide on the right wine to go with roast goose or with egg foo yung. But there was a way out of the dilemma.

'I'd like you, Selena, to teach me how to drive a man wild, using Rupert as our test subject.'

Selena's eyes widened. She nodded, thoughtfully. 'Tease our Rupert? Excellent choice, Connie, fun and educational at the same time.'

'So,' Connie asked, 'do we get dressed up first?'

Selena shook her head. 'I don't think so. We've seen you walk and sit. You wear heels well and know how to pose your body, both walking and seated. It's obvious that you know how to dress seductively.'

Connie gave Tina silent thanks.

Selena continued. 'Let's consider moves that work whether you are dressed or naked, shall we? Some body-language and some "contact" moves?'

'"Contact-moves" sounds interesting.'

Rupert said, 'Skip the body-language for now, Selena. She's a natural at that. All she needs is to become aware of what she already does by instinct.'

Selena laughed. 'You're just in a rush for us girls to get our hands on you, my love.'

'I won't deny that.'

'Just our hands on him?' Connie asked as innocently as she could.

Rupert grinned. 'If ever I met a natural flirt, you are her, little Connie.'

She blushed.

Selena said, 'Let's start with "visual flirtation for the naked".'

Connie almost laughed. 'That sounds like a college course, "Naked Flirtation 101".'

'It'd be a popular one, I think,' Rupert added. 'If they'd offered it in my day, I'd have taken it.'

'The human eye follows movement,' Selena explained. 'If there are a lot of naked bodies around, as in an orgy, people's eyes are drawn to what moves.'

'So I should wave my breasts in the air?'

'Silly. People move their hands when they talk, most of us. So, while you discuss the price of cabbages or the latest celebrity scandal, as your hand passes in front of your body, just a subtle touch, like this …' As her fingers passed her left nipple, they brushed over it without pausing. 'That brings eyes to your nipples. If that proves to be too understated, wet your fingertips and let them pause and roll your nipple, just for a second.'

'And if that doesn't work, give it a good hard tweak?'

'Why not, if that's what it takes?' Selena got up and went to a divan, where she lay full length, one thigh crossed over the other in a classical pose. 'The same goes for your pussy, Connie. Brush across it unobtrusively or, better yet, just lie like this.' She draped a hand across the line of her groin, fingertips just resting on where the lips of her pussy met, and slid the very tip of one between them. 'The secret here is *not* to play with yourself. Just let your finger rest there. Anyone watching you will expect some sort of masturbation, even if it's just a tiny stroking. After watching you *not*masturbating for a while, they'll become impatient. Anticipation, you see?'

'I see. Are you going to …?'

'Play with myself?'

'Yes.'

'No. Doesn't that make you want to play with me?'

'Yes.'

'How about this, then?' Selena pushed down on her own mound with one finger and dipped another into her own slit before pulling it up, exposing the head of her large clitoris.

Connie cleared her throat. 'I hadn't realised that you are so big down there,' she said.

Selena rotated a fingertip on her clit's head. 'Does that make you want to suck on it?'

'Yes.'

'Did you see what my words did to Rupert? Even though he's fully erect, my suggestion that you go down on me made his cock twitch. See how two women can work on a man together? Come over here.' Selena swung her feet to the floor and sat upright on the divan.

Connie sat beside her.

'Now, we don't spread or do anything crude,' Selena explained, 'but if you rest your hand in my lap and if you tuck the very tip of a finger into me – yes, like that – and I do the same to you, like this, how do you think us just sitting here like this makes Rupert feel?'

'Horny as hell,' he said.

'I have to tell you, Connie,' Selena continued, 'about one evening early in my relationship with dear Rupert. It was at a dinner party – just a regular party – not an orgy or anything, but all sophisticated people. I was sat next to a cute little redhead.'

'Veronica,' Rupert supplied.

'With Rupert at the head of the table, next to me. I contrived to drop a fork under the table. Rupert, being a gentleman, bent under the table to retrieve it. Well, my skirt was high-slit and Veronica's dress was very short. We each had a fingertip tucked into the other's pussy. The look that Rupert gave to Veronica and me when he emerged from under the table – you could have branded a herd of cattle with it!'

'My sweet harlot,' Rupert almost purred. 'That's the first indication I had from you two that you *both* wanted to go home with me.'

'I think that's one of the secrets to our relationship,' Selena continued. 'We tease each other every chance we get.'

'It keeps your lust fresh,' Connie guessed.

'Just like Selena is teasing me now. She's talking sex and showing me sex, but I still am not getting any physical sex.'

'You poor man,' said Connie sympathetically.

'I'm not complaining,' he explained. 'Drag it out as long as you like, you two. Don't

complain if I spontaneously combust, though.'

'In that case ...' Selena said. She twisted towards Connie and wrapped an arm around her waist to pull her closer. 'Watch this!' Her lips paused a fraction of an inch from Connie's. Selena's tongue lapped out. Its tip slowly circled the insides of Connie's lips, keeping enough distance between their mouths that her moving tongue was visible to Rupert.

Connie liked this game. She extended her own tongue in turn, to slither over Serena's and make its own slow circuits.

Rupert grunted.

'He likes it,' Selena breathed into Connie's mouth. 'I can tell.'

'True,' he agreed. 'Tease away, ladies! Torment me! Be merciless!'

Selena cupped Connie's warm left breast. Her thumb's ball smoothed over her nipple.

'You two are *so* hot together,' Rupert said.

How many times had she kissed women, now? Connie wondered. Was this the fourth, or fifth? It couldn't be many but already she was learning a new pleasure that she could derive from it – kissing another woman while a man watched them with open admiration. Being lusted after was like – like a wild fire, igniting every erotic atom in her body.

Would Selena watching her kiss Rupert be as effective? No. Exciting but not so intensely. After all, Selena had watched her and Rupert fuck, and that had been a major thrill but less of a forbidden one and that made a difference.

No wonder showing herself off turned her on so. Her mother had made it such a major taboo.

Selena's kisses were getting to her. Her thighs were squirming together.

'You know what else turns Rupert on when he watches?'

'Do tell!'

Selena twisted and fell onto her back, pulling Connie on top of her. By instinct, Connie ground down, pubes on pubes.

'Like this,' Selena told her. 'Sit up a bit.' She took Connie's right leg and folded it up with its foot beside her waist. Her left leg was spread wide and drooping to the floor. With their thighs parted wide, pubes on pubes, Selena ground up, moving her hips in long slow circles.

Connie could feel her friend's soft wet lips being folded, then parted and stretched, then, for a brief moment, Selena's clitoris flipping between the lips of Connie's pussy.

'Oh yes!' Connie said, and humped.

'Frottage,' Selena told her. 'Pussy-on-pussy. Can you feel how hot and wet I am, Connie?'

'We could climax this way,' Connie observed with an extra twitch of her hips.

'We certainly could. Rupert, what do you think? You want me to fuck our dear little Connie till she comes all over my pussy?'

'And your Selena squirts all over mine?' Connie added.

'You'd do that, just to tease me?' Rupert said, dryly. 'How could I refuse such a selfless sacrifice? You spoil me! Take your time, dear ladies. We've lots of it.'

Connie squirmed harder. Where the lips of her sex were splayed over Selena's, there was a delightful warm wetness. She inhaled deeply to suck in the clean sweet lemony musk. Her mouth watered. It needed ... She turned her head to see that Rupert was up off the bed and crossing to them. His cock stood out before him like the prow of a proud ship. Was he going to give it to her mouth? She hadn't sucked on a man since Jeff walked out on her. She watched the wagging knob as if it was a hypnotist's watch being swayed before her eyes.

But no. Nor did he offer it to Selena. He bent over Connie and put his lips on hers. She was the one to give in to temptation. She reached out sideways to take a grip on his shaft and hold it while his expert tongue explored her mouth and drank of its nectar. By reflex, she pumped on his thick column. A tiny drop of clear fluid dripped from his cock's eye and splattered Selena's breast. Smiling, the older woman scooped the dewdrop on a fingertip and held it up. Connie took her mouth from Rupert's for just long enough to suck Selena's fingertip dry.

'Oh fuck!' Connie exclaimed. 'You two have got me crazy horny. I thought we were teasing Rupert, Selena, but I've *got* to come, please?'

Selena said, 'Teasing can backfire, can't it? I know that when I make other people horny, it makes me horny too. Rupert, my love, shall we take mercy on the poor girl? We can continue her lessons after.'

'Of course, lovey.' He scooped Connie up as effort-lessly as if she'd been a baby, strode across the room and deposited her on the bed. Standing beside her, he looked down and said, 'Connie, your aroma is delicious.'

'Thank you.'

He took her ankles, lifted them, spun her round on her bottom and dragged her behind to the edge of the bed. 'I *have* to have some,' he announced, and dropped to his knees. His big hands lifted Connie beneath her thighs and set them on his broad shoulders, bracketing his head. 'You're glistening wet down here,' he told her. 'Some of it has to be yours, and some my Selena's. What an intoxicating cocktail!'

Connie hitched herself up onto her elbows so that she could watch Rupert. As far as she could tell, looking at his face as he gazed so intently at her sex, he was really adoring her pussy. That was flattering and somehow quite touching, on a number of levels. All her life, she'd been trained to abhor the sight of her own sexual parts. She'd been taught to detest and be ashamed of everything that made her a woman.

Oh, Mother! How could you have been so wrong for your entire life?

103

Talking to the entire universe, Connie declared, 'I am a woman!'

'Oh yes,' Rupert agreed. He took a long lap in the crease of Connie's groin, from her hip down to below her sex, then another down the other side.

Selena knelt on the bed beside Connie's head and tucked a pillow up under it to make it easier for her to watch what Rupert did to her.

He returned to the base of her slit, just below where her lips met. She had to be dribbling down there. The tip of his tongue twitched from side to side, tantalising skin that was so much more sensitive since the waxing. His thumbs pressed at either side of her sex, parting its lips, opening her up like some lush tropical fruit. His tongue explored in there, dipping into the tiny cup where her sex's lips met, pushing the pulpiness of those lips to one side and then the other, squirming and straining to penetrate her deeply. All the time, she could feel a gentle suction pulling the liquor of her lust into his mouth.

It was so beautiful. Not just the sensations, but what she could see and envision of what he did. For the most part, his mouth was out of sight, nuzzling into her, but the angles that he held his head at, combined with what she could feel, gave her a mental image of what was concealed from her eyes. It was as if Rupert was memorising every inch of the inside of her sex: the soft and yielding, the hard smoothness where thin flesh was stretched over bone, the labyrinthine intricacies where she was convoluted.

Was she pink, in there? In part, for sure, but were there other shades? She'd learned so much about herself, and about her sex, so quickly, but she'd still never seen inside herself. She put it on her to-do list.

Selena leaned over her. 'Wine?'

'Please.'

The woman emptied her glass into her own mouth, bent low, put her lips to Connie's and let the wine dribble from her mouth into the younger woman's. The sharing of it diluted it, of course, but diluted it was twice as heady as before.

Oh! Rupert's tongue had reached her clit, finally. It worked, deftly but gently, easing its hood back. He sucked air, cooling it, and blew to warm it again. His tongue slavered, soaking the sensitive little polyp. A finger joined his tongue, folding the lip of her sex over her clit's head, covering its upper left quadrant. How did he know that was the most sensitive area? Was there some sign he'd read in her, or was it the same with all women? She'd have to ask.

His tongue moved, sliding half over her clit's head, half over the skin that shielded it. That was good. Too hard and direct made her uncomfortable at times but the way he was doing it, she could endure an awful lot of it.

Selena gave her more mouth-to-mouth wine and toyed with Connie's left nipple.

Connie swallowed and asked, 'You said you'd come in my mouth, Selena. Please?'

'You're such a greedy little bitch, Connie,' Selena said. 'Of course I'll come in your mouth, as you ask so nicely.'

Selena put the wine bottle aside, but close at hand. She stepped over Connie and lowered herself until her sex was just above Connie's face and she was kneeling astride her.

Connie stared up. Selena's lips were parted but not enough for her to be able to see far inside. She *could* detect different shades of pink, though.

The woman hitched herself into position and slid two fingertips into herself. She pulled back, popping her engorged clit into the open air. Her sheath had retracted, leaving clit-head and shaft fully exposed. She gripped the stalk behind its head between two knuckles. That wouldn't have been comfortable for Connie, but ... The phrase 'Different strokes for different folks' came into her head and she grinned.

'Tongue, flat,' Selena demanded.

Connie extended her tongue, spread to its fullest width. It was hard to focus that close up but she felt Selena push down on her clit and rub its head on the flat of her tongue. Then there was liquid pouring. Oh – it wasn't Selena's climax, of course, not yet, it was wine. She was lubricating the movement of her clit on Connie's tongue by pouring wine over where they met.

Connie let wine, slightly flavoured by the aroma of Selena's sex, trickle into her mouth and down her throat.

Connie closed her eyes. Trying to focus that close-up was tiring them. In any case, she wanted to concentrate on what she was feeling.

There was Rupert's tongue, seemingly tireless, lapping steadily at her clit. He'd worked a couple of fingers into her and was palpitating her engorged lips from their insides. Then there was Selena's clit, being rubbed on the flat of her tongue.

She was being used as a sex-object, she realised. That was politically incorrect, but did the statue of Aphrodite that was reproduced a hundred times around the Gran Playa feel slighted by being admired as a work of erotic art? No. Nor did Connie feel insulted because her physical self was giving pleasure to her dear new friends.

She was proud to be lusted after.

They had to feel proud that she lusted for them.

There is no shame in lust, whether you feel it yourself or inspire it in others. It is modesty, the denial of pleasure, that is shameful.

Connie wanted to proclaim the feeling of triumph that washed over her but her tongue was being put to far better use. She made an involuntary little mewing sound.

'You OK?' Selena asked.

Connie nodded, but gently, not to dislodge Selena's clit.

Selena said, 'I'm getting close, you two. Ready when you are, Rupert.'

The fingers that were inside Connie slithered up higher, behind her pubic bone, and began to palpitate her G-spot. His tongue's movements accelerated.

Selena gasped, 'You're making me come, Connie darling. You are such a sexy little slut, my dear. You're bursting with lust. You should share it.' Her voice became incoherent, just breathy babbling. Her fingers frigged harder and faster.

'Oh, Connie! Oh, Connie!' She was almost screaming. Her thighs, bracketing Connie, began to shiver, then shake, then jerk uncontrollably.

'Yes!' she bellowed.

Her come splattered Connie's face and into her mouth but she was prepared and swallowed quickly, though she would have liked the time to savour the woman-dew.

Whether it was knowing what she'd done to Selena or whether Rupert did something different, Connie wasn't sure, but she went tight all over, screwed up to the breaking point, and relaxed, absolutely, letting a series of delicious little orgasms flow out of her body.

Selena was husky when she said, 'Thank you, Connie. That was very nice. Now, just a short break, maybe, and then we really *must* do something about Rupert's erection, before it becomes permanent.'

Chapter Thirteen

Connie and Selena shared a shower while Rupert phoned out for supper. Inevitably, it was playful but with no urgency. Neither of them was seducing the other. That there would be more sex between them that evening was taken for granted, though not unappreciated. Slippery palms took longer than necessary to soap hard nipples. Selena washed Connie's sex and behind, one hand on each, but even when the tip of Selena's right index finger slipped between the lips of Connie's sex and the tip of her left index finger barely penetrated her behind, it was pleasant without being urgent. It did bring anal sex to Connie's mind. Jeff had been particularly fond of taking her that way but neither of her new lovers had shown particular interest in penetrating her there, or of being penetrated by her that way.

Perhaps it didn't interest them particularly. She hoped that wasn't the case. There was something about being sodomised, apart from the physical sensations, something deep and dark, emotionally, that she'd like to investigate again further, and soon.

There was so much about sex to explore, wasn't there? Somehow, a lifetime didn't seem long enough.

The shower play turned a little more intense when Selena kissed Connie deeply while lifting and rubbing her soapy wet thigh between hers. That, Connie realised, was because the games were about to be put on pause while they ate and Selena wanted to keep her libidinous.

Tease! To retaliate, hugging Selena, she ran a finger down the crease between her bum cheeks and let it linger for just a fraction of a second, rimming her sphincter.

Connie skipped out of the shower too quickly for Selena's wild swat to land.

There were little towelling skirts with Velcro fasteners waiting, draped over a heated towel rail. Connie could get used to this sort of sybaritic life. The two women sat side-by-side at a jade marble vanity to fix their makeup.

'I know that it'll be a mess again in no time,' Selena explained, 'but ...'

'Rupert is worth it,' Connie finished for her.

Selena held up her lipstick. 'Crimson Passion,' she said. 'It's OK on me but it looks *really* good as a ring around Rupert's cock.'

Connie laughed. 'In that case, might I borrow it?'

While Rupert took his shower, the women laid the dining room table with regular knives and forks, lobster picks, lobster crackers and some long, thin, very delicate two-pronged barbed forks. Selena opened a pinot gris and turned a magnum of Dom Pérignon in a stainless-steel ice bucket filled with salted ice.

'Cools faster,' Selena explained about the salt.

Their feast was delivered by a golf cart marked 'Chez Aphrodite'. Rupert was still showering so the two women lugged the hamper in with the aid of a cute blonde in a diaphanous Greek chiton. The girl looked at Selena and Connie, topless, with admiration and no disapproval.

'All this, for three of us?' Connie asked.

'Rupert doesn't know what you like in the way of seafood so, to be sure, he'd have ordered a wide variety.'

'He's very generous.'

'Yes, he is, in every way.'

There was a platter of assorted sushi, pickled seaweed, a rice, shrimp and broccoli dish, lobster thermidor, three whole boiled lobsters, a basket of King Crab legs, a Dungeness crab, a giant dish of oysters on the half shell, two shellfish that Connie didn't recognise and something jellied or in aspic. The bread was sourdough and still warm from the oven, with sweet butter waiting.

Selena poured wine just as Rupert returned, in a male version of the skirts they were wearing, freshly shaven and with his hair still damp.

Selena said, 'I see that erection of yours is still with us.'

'It's very patient, lovey.'

'Show us.'

He parted his brief garment. His cock wasn't quite as stiff as it had been earlier but it hadn't softened much.

Selena gave it a brief stroke. 'There, there. Selena and Connie will take good care of you.' She paused. 'After supper.'

Rupert told her that she was a teasing bitch and kissed her cheek.

Forty minutes later, the still wine had been drunk, the table was littered with shells and empty crab legs, half a loaf had disappeared and all three of them had greasy faces and hands. The women went to the bathroom to repair their makeup while Rupert cleared away. They were at the vanity trying perfumes when he appeared carrying the ice bucket and the champagne.

'Don't spray that stuff anywhere I might put my mouth,' he warned.

'We were just saying the same thing,' Selena told him. 'So far, the only safe place we've thought of is in our hair.'

'I brought the champagne up,' he said. 'I was wondering if Connie has ever tried Dom Pérignon our way.'

'What way is that?' Connie asked.

'We should demonstrate for her, my love,' Selena told Rupert.

'That's why I brought the bottle.'

He untwisted the wire with meticulous care and then stripped the foil off. Connie expected the usual thumbs-and-pop but he worked and twisted and eased the cork until it fell into his palm without the slightest drop of foam following.

'I'll go first,' Selena said. 'Then Connie will know what to expect.'

Rupert took a cloth and wiped all around the neck of the bottle. Selena dropped her towelling skirt, hitched her bottom up onto the vanity and lifted one foot up onto a stool. Rupert moved another stool over to support her other foot, so that her legs were wide apart.

Their intent was obvious, and fascinating. 'Are you really going to …?' Connie asked. 'Can you get drunk that way?'

'You most certainly can,' Rupert told her, 'and it's quicker than the other way. It's best not to overindulge.' He squatted between Selena's feet, holding the magnum in both hands.

Selena parted the lips of her sex for him. Connie bent closer, not to miss a thing. The rim of the bottle nudged its way between Selena's pussy lips. It wasn't even as thick as Rupert's cock, not until it flared out lower, so the insertion was easy. With about two and a half inches actually inside his woman, he rocked the bottle gently.

'Yes, it's coming,' Selena said, her voice taut.

Connie bent even closer, her eyes glued to the lips of Selena's pussy where they clung to the glass.

'Yes!' Selena squealed.

Foam fizzed out between the bottle and her clinging

lips. Rupert pulled the bottle back and clamped his mouth over his woman's sex. His thumb sealed the bottle. His gulps and sucking were so noisy, he had to be exaggerating for effect, and it *was* effective. Connie found the sight and sound of Rupert sucking champagne from Selena's body extraordinarily arousing.

At last, he slurped back and licked his lips. 'Delicious!' he declared. 'Would you like some, Connie?'

'Would I!'

He slipped the bottle back into Selena and gave it a little shake.

'Here it comes!' Selena warned. A little squirt jetted out between her flesh and the glass.

Rupert pulled the bottle out. Connie spread her lips over Selena's mound. Bubbles foamed into her mouth, crisp still but not as cold as champagne should be served, not that Connie cared about that. She drank until no more wine flowed, then sucked.

Selena hitched off the vanity. 'Your turn, Connie.'

'My ...?'

'For a champagne douche. Don't you want to try it?'

'Of course I do, please. Lots of it.'

'Not enough to get you drunk,' Rupert chided. 'A little wine drunk with sex can be delightful but sex with a drunk is nothing but a pain.'

'No, I didn't mean that you should get me drunk, Rupert,' Connie explained. 'I wouldn't want that.'

'Of course you wouldn't. We three get drunk enough on lust, don't we? OK, Connie, your turn. Up on the vanity.'

She climbed up and parted the lips of her sex, ready. The bottle's neck wasn't even cold, going in. It had been warmed by Selena's body-heat. 'I'm ready,' she said.

She felt the bottle jiggle and then the rush of foam, almost like diving into a too cool sea, but in reverse – the sea washing into her. She could feel it gushing and swirling into her, rinsing through her, filling her pussy – invading her.

And Selena's mouth was over her sex, sucking, and the tide subsided and drained from her.

'Wow!' she said. 'That was different. Too bad you we can't give you a turn, Rupert.'

Selena looked up at her with wine dripping from her mouth. 'But we can, Connie, in a way.'

'Huh? How?'

'Like this.' Selena took the bottle in one hand and knelt at Rupert's feet. Her free hand gripped his shaft.

What on earth? How was she expecting to get the wine into …?

Selena tilted her head back, opened her mouth wide and poured the wine between her own lips, filling her mouth until it brimmed. She steered Rupert's cock down until its head was submerged. Her lips formed a tight seal around his shaft. Rupert flexed, pushing down into the champagne that filled her mouth.

115

Felix Baron

'It feels fizzy,' he said. 'I don't know if it feels to me the way having your pussies filled with it does to you, but it's certainly a very interesting sensation.'

Selena nodded and shook her head. A little champagne squirted out beside his shaft. He pumped, short, tightly controlled movements, fucking into her mouth. From the expression on his face, he was finding the sensations *very* pleasant.

'Are you going to come?' Connie asked him. 'Are you going to make a champagne cocktail for her?'

He said, 'No,' but his voice was strained.

Selena tugged at Connie's arm. She didn't understand but she let herself be drawn down to Selena's level. Selena's free hand was pumping at Rupert's shaft now, as if she rejected his decision not to reach his climax.

Rupert said, 'I see. Very well.' His movements accelerated.

Selena pulled Connie's face close to her own.

'Now!' Rupert said. He thrust into Selena's mouth, deeper and faster. 'Yes!'

He jerked and froze. Selena, lips sealed, twisted her head to bring her mouth to Connie's. Understanding, Connie opened wide to accept the stream of wine mixed with Rupert's juices that jetted into her mouth.

Selena explained, 'I wanted Rupert to climax, Connie, so that I can show you how I get him erect and ready again.'

116

Chapter Fourteen

Selena made lobster and mayonnaise sandwiches and wrapped them to be ready for when anyone got hungry again. 'Wasn't that fun?' she asked Connie.

'Wild. I can't thank you and Rupert enough. All the time and effort you two are taking over my education and amusement.'

'We've taken quite a shine to you, Connie. You know that.' She laid a hand on Connie's arm. 'Connie, have you ever thought about a career acting?'

'Acting? Like on the stage?'

'Or like on television.'

'No, why do you ask?'

'Something about you. We get the impression you might be good at it.'

'Even if I were, it's hard to make a living that way, right?'

'Not necessarily.'

'Are you and Rupert theatre people then?'

'Not exactly.' She shook her head. 'I've said too much. Forget I spoke.'

'Curiouser and curiouser.'

'OK, Alice in Wonderland, let's go construct ourselves an erection.'

'And then demolish it again.'

'Of course.'

Arm in arm, they went upstairs to the bedroom where Rupert, with no erection, was waiting. His tanned body was sprawled face-down across the bed like a bronze statue. He snored ostentatiously, twice.

'Poor old man,' Selena said. 'It seems we've worn him out.'

'Shame.'

'Well, he's not getting any younger. I should start looking for a really nice rocking chair for him and think about hiring him a nurse.'

'A naughty nurse, of course.'

'Not too naughty, not for his declining years. The strain, you know.'

'And I was so looking forward to my lesson in how best to get Rupert horny. I guess that from here on it'll have to be left to Viagra.'

'Extra strength, at that.' Selena went to the dressing table. 'While we have him, he really doesn't take proper care of himself so we should take the opportunity to cream his skin.'

'We won't wake him up?'

'No, he's out like a light.'

Rupert snored again.

Selena picked up a big pink pot. 'Would you mind giving me a hand, Connie? There's such a lot of him that otherwise I could be at it all night if I do it all on my own.' She stifled a fake sob. 'I can remember when "at it all night" meant something entirely different, where Rupert was concerned. There was a time he'd go through the entire chorus line of the *Folies Bergère* and still have enough left over for a pair of Chinese contortionists.'

'How the mighty have fallen!'

'Indeed!' Selena took a scoop from her jar and passed it to Connie. 'If you'll do that side?'

'Certainly.'

They started with his calves, smoothing and kneading and slowly working their way higher.

'Nice thighs,' Connie commented.

'Powerful, in their day. Lots of stamina. What do you think of his bum?'

Both dug their knuckles into Rupert's hard muscles.

'Nice,' Connie said. 'You know, Selena, just because he's asleep, it doesn't mean that I have to miss my lesson. You could still tell me and show me, even if he isn't up to reacting.'

'True.' She slapped Rupert's right cheek. 'And this would be an excellent place to start.'

'I kind of thought it might be.'

Selena produced a cloth and wiped the excess cream off Rupert's muscular buttocks. She climbed onto the bed and knelt between her lover's thighs. The heel of her hand rotated on his coccyx. 'This area, the base of his spine, is quite sensitive. You can get nice results from stroking it, like this' – her fingertips drifted over his skin – 'or by using the tip of your tongue, like this ...' She demonstrated. 'Or by nibbling gently.' Her small white teeth took a gentle grip.

Rupert's left cheek flexed. The women looked into each other's eyes with amusement.

'May I try?' Connie asked.

'By all means.'

Connie stroked, then licked, then nibbled. Rupert might have made a little sound, deep in his throat, but they couldn't be sure.

'How about this ...?' Connie asked. She bore down, one hand flat on each buttock, and eased them apart. Her tongue worked over the lump of his tailbone, and lower, into the crease. Connie held a finger up and rotated it in the air while looking a question at Selena. The older woman shook her head and poked her own tongue out to touch its tip with a finger. Connie nodded.

Her tongue squirmed lower until it crossed the perimeter of his ring and lapped at the striated skin there. Without intending to, she dribbled.

Selena said, 'Yes, if he was awake and aware, he'd be enjoying that. May I show you how I do it?'

'Of course, Selena. You're the tutor here. I want to learn all I can.'

When Selena demonstrated, her tongue's tip spiralled around the perimeter of Rupert's knot, stiffened and prodded. There was definitely a responsive sound from deep in the man's chest but the women chose to ignore it.

'If he was awake,' Selena said, 'he'd be keeping us busy about now but, as he's fast asleep, we can continue with creaming his skin for him.'

'Taking advantage of the circumstances,' Connie observed.

'Exactly.'

Kneeling to each side of Rupert, they creamed and massaged, working their way higher, over his waist, his lower back, shoulder blades, to his shoulders.

'You know,' Selena said, 'even when Rupert is the done-to rather than the doer, he still likes to fondle me as I pleasure him, even if it's just cupping my breast. What I mean is, if he were awake right now, he'd be like this, most likely.' She pulled Rupert's wrist up between her thighs, tucked two of his fingers into her sex and squeezed her legs together to hold his hand there.

'I see,' Connie said. 'Like this?'

'Exactly. I find it kind of pleasant, don't you?'

121

'I do. Thank you for the lesson, Selena.' Despite his being 'sound asleep', Rupert's fingers wriggled a little inside her. Connie felt herself leaking onto his hand. She worked on his deltoids with renewed vigour. 'I like to have the back of my neck nibbled,' Connie told her friend. 'Does he like that?'

'I really don't know. I'll be sure to find out next time I make love with him – when he's awake, I mean. Thank you for the suggestion.'

'You're welcome. Well, that's his back done. How do we turn him over?'

'Yes, he's quite a weight. This should work, though. Get off the bed for a moment.'

Connie followed Selena's lead. They untucked the sheets, got a grip on the bottom one with all four hands and pulled as they lifted. Rupert rolled over.

'Well done us,' Selena said. She looked down at Rupert. 'I think it'll be easier if we spread him out a bit more, don't you?'

'I see what you mean. One leg at a time?'

'Easiest.' They took his right ankle and pulled it over as far as they could. Then his left in the opposite direction. 'Looks kind of vulnerable like that, doesn't he,' Selena observed.

'Sweet, with it.'

'Particularly …' Selena waved a hand in the general direction of his genitals. His testicles lay on the sheet, so full and large that it seemed impossible that he ever crossed his legs. His cock, a limp curve but slightly thickened now, was draped across his left thigh.

'Yummy,' Connie remarked.

'They are rather nice, aren't they, cocks,' Selena agreed.

'Particularly that one.'

'Why, thank you, Connie. I'm sure that your boyfriend who you might get back with some day has a very handsome one as well.'

'Thanks. Selena, as this one is handy, as it were, could you continue my lesson? Who knows, we might convince it to become an erection even while Rupert sleeps. Men wake up with hard-ons, so they must get them in their sleep sometimes, right?'

'Of course, Connie, and apart from enjoying creating them, I also love to watch the process. It's kind of magical, to me.'

'So teach me to abracadabra.'

'Let's bend his legs up then, so that we can get to him properly.'

Two women to a leg, one at a time, they moved Rupert's feet up the bed, soles planted flat. Somehow, miraculously, he stayed in that position when they let go.

Selena lay on the bed, face up close to Rupert's scrotum. 'Can you see OK?' she asked.

'Pretty good.'

'Could you lift his balls up for me, gently?'

123

Felix Baron

'Of course.' Connie found it hard not to giggle as she inserted the back of her hand under Rupert's bulging sac and eased his balls higher.

Selena wriggled in closer. 'I'm going to lick his bum-hole and behind his balls,' she explained.

'I can remember that.' Connie scrunched down to get as close a view as possible. 'It's dark down there but I can see pretty well. Selena, you're having an effect on his cock as well. Look at that! It's growing thicker and longer and lifting up off his leg. Isn't that fascinating?'

'Huh-huh!'

'It's standing up now. My goodness! Amazing, huh? Selena, would you mind, now that you've managed to give him an erection, even in his sleep, would it be OK by you if I sucked on it?'

'Minute!' Selena pulled back far enough that she could talk. 'Before you suck, look at the underside of his shaft.'

'Right.'

'See where his foreskin is attached, just below his cock's head, like a little knot in his skin?'

'I see it.'

'Lick him there. Use the very tip of your tongue. Men *love* that. With you tantalising him there and me working on him behind his balls, well, who knows what might happen to our Sleeping Prince.'

'Got it!' With one hand cupping Rupert's balls and the other fist wrapped around his shaft, her head resting on his thigh, Connie extended her tongue and did as Selena had described.

Selena made little pleased grunts as she worked on her man's perineum and anus. From time to time Rupert twitched but, if he was awake, he wasn't revealing it, or didn't until Connie began to pump on his shaft. Finally, he let out a loud grunt.

Connie moved her attention from his knot and covered his cock's helmet with her mouth. Her tongue pushed up on the same knot she'd been tantalising but this time to push his glans up against the ridges of her palate. She nodded, hard.

Rupert burst out, 'Oh fuck!' His legs lifted his rump off the bed.

Selena commanded him, 'No! Hold it, Rupert, please. Don't let it go!'

Shivering with the effort, he subsided and slowly relaxed, one set of muscles at a time, though his shaft was still quivering.

'What's the matter, Selena?' Connie asked.

'One, I wanted to show off Rupert's *incredible* self-control. Can you imagine the willpower that took? Two, I have one last lesson planned for you today, Connie, and I need Rupert to be erect for me to teach it to you.'

'Bitch!' Rupert said.

'You love it,' she responded.

'True. So what comes next?'

125

'Could you fetch the footstool, please, my love?'

'Oh – that. I sure can.' He got off the bed.

Selena told Connie, 'This is a matter of geometry.'

'Geometry?'

'Angles. In particular, angles of forty-five degrees and ninety degrees.'

'Now I'm confused,' Connie confessed.

'All will be made clear to you,' Selena promised.

Rupert set a footstool that was a little taller than average down beside the bed.

'Could you kneel on that, please, Connie?' Selena asked.

'Sure.' Connie got off the bed and dropped her knees onto the stool's padded top.

'Hands on floor. Please?'

Connie obeyed.

'Elbows on the floor, I think. I want your back to slope at forty-five degrees.'

'I'm intrigued.'

'Math was never like this at school, right? OK, head down, face resting on your forearms. More like this.' Selena guided her friend's body. 'Good, exactly like that.'

'Look at Rupert's cock. What angle would you say it stands up at?'

It wasn't exactly so but Connie gave the answer she guessed that Selena wanted: 'Forty-five degrees.'

'Right. Rupert, my love, you know what to do next.'

'I think I can remember,' he said with a chuckle. He took a position behind Connie. With her kneeling on a high stool, her sex was almost exactly at the same level as his cock. He entered her easily. He was very hard and she was saturated inside already.

'You see,' Selena explained, 'with his cock sloping up at forty-five degrees and your vagina sloping down at forty-five degrees, he's entering you at exactly ninety degrees.'

'Which is impossible,' Connie said.

'Not if you force it, it isn't. Push, Rupert!'

Rupert pushed. The rear wall of her vagina forced his shaft down, exerting the maximum slippery pressure. Under this tension, the underside of his cock was pressed hard against her pubic bone and her clitoral shaft.

'Oh, I see what you mean,' Connie gasped.

'Fuck her, Rupert,' Selena ordered.

'With pleasure.' He began pumping, His cock was so much stronger than Connie's insides that it distorted her to conform with its shape, all the while applying maximum pressure to her most sensitive areas. The stimulation was excruciatingly intense, and then Selena slid a wet finger into Connie's anus.

Connie wasn't sure what happened next. It felt that a maelstrom was consuming her from the inside out. If she could see, she wasn't aware of what she saw. If she heard, it was with deaf ears. Her thoughts were nothing, intensely nothing. The next thing she knew, her head was cradled against Connie's soft breast and Rupert was standing above the two of them with warm semen dripping from his cock's eye onto her tummy.

Selena cleared her throat. 'Anyone for lobster sandwiches?'

Chapter Fifteen

The phone beside Connie's bed chirped.

Selena said, 'Rupert and I are developing tan-lines from sunning at the pool. We plan to spend a day at the beach to fix that. You up for it?'

'Nude?'

'We have a locker at the snack bar. Nude from there.'

Connie had her 'Daisy' outfit that she hadn't tried on yet and was eager to. Going to the beach meant that she'd only get to wear it to and from but that was OK. She showered and was very careful to dry herself thoroughly. Strip-Tack wouldn't work on damp skin. The bikini comprised two thin strips of fabric, each with a cloth daisy at each end. She stuck one daisy onto her pubes, low enough to cover clit and slit, drew the strip between her legs, pulled it up between the cheeks of her bum at the back like a thong and stuck the other daisy over her tailbone. The bra she draped over the back of her neck, lifted her breasts slightly and stuck the daisies to her nipples, like pasties. It provided uplift without restricting the way she swayed.

Connie had matching sandals and a square of gauze with a daisy pattern. When it was folded into a triangle and wrapped low around her hips, the ends of the gauze didn't quite meet so she stuck them in place, leaving a three-inch gap of bare skin to puzzle and intrigue observers. The final touch was an oversized broad-brim black straw hat, with three daisies as trimming.

Rupert and Selena had their own golf cart. They met her outside her building and whisked her away to the beach. Rupert was dressed down and looking quite piratical in nothing but clinging black jeans. Selena's outfit was similarly basic, just a floral sarong that could be worn as either a short dress or a long skirt. She'd knotted it just beneath her cute little breasts, to make neither. It was made out of chiffon. With the light behind it, it was virtually invisible.

Rupert opened one of the lockers that were built into the outside wall of the snack bar. They stripped naked and stowed their stuff.

Rupert said, 'Ah, there they are.' He led the way to a spot on the beach where four of the resort staff were setting up three loungers and a couple of umbrellas plus a table with a gigantic hamper.

'I see that we're roughing it today, Rupert,' said Connie.

He grinned. 'The snack bar is all out of caviar and all you can get from the booze bar here is beer, sangria and those coconut things with umbrellas that Selena likes so much. I'm not fussy. A good scotch, a fine cognac or a really dry Beefeater martini and I'm happy, but there are limits to the hardships I'm willing to endure.'

'Snob!' Selena accused.

He was handed a martini by a server and passed a roll of notes back. 'Thanks, Renaldo. That'll be it for the day, thanks.' To Connie, he said, 'The hat worked for you, by the way.'

'It did?'

'You drew more stares with it on than you would have without it, I promise you.'

'I'm sure that you're right. I feel barer with it than I would without it, as well.'

'Your bald pussy is being admired, as well.'

Connie preened. 'It is? Who by?'

'Apart from me? Look my way, beyond me, three more loungers over, naked but in a red bathing cap.'

'The one with the face two sizes too small for her head and very tall ankles instead of legs?'

'Even the plain can yearn, Connie. Lust is a democracy.'

'Of course they can. I hope she gets a kick out of looking at me, but how do we know it isn't you she's ogling?'

'She's in a suite with two girlfriends. I think that's kind of nice. They can wander around all day getting their boilers stoked by all the succulent beauty on display, then retire to their suite for some of the hot and heavy stuff. That's very economical. The stimulus is being shared out among the less fortunate.'

'In economics, we call it the trickle-down effect.'

'Trickle down their legs?'

'Rupert!'

'Sorry. May I pour you a drink to make up for my crudeness?'

'Not just now, thanks. Later, for sure. For now, I'm going to check out some of that beauty for myself.' She pulled an oversized pair of mirror sunglasses from her bag and put them on. 'Can you tell who I'm looking at when I wear these?'

'No, you're in the clear.'

'It's a little trick I learned from you and Selena on the day we met.'

'Why, so you did. You've come a long way, Connie.'

'In such a short time, as well.'

'That's because, deep down inside, where it really, really counts, you've been evil all along.'

'You've got a point there.' She sank down onto her lounger and let her head loll to one side so she'd look as if she were dozing while she was spying.

'Rupert?' she asked after a while.

'Yes?'

'What are the rules on the beach, about sex and stuff?'

'It's more customs than rules but full nudity is fine and so are brief displays of affection but fucking in public is considered bad manners unless the fuckers are very discreet. Some people make use of the showers. They've room for two. That's mainly very casual sex, though – when people are struck by sudden lust and don't want to wait for introductions.'

'Like the couple next to me?'

Rupert sat up to reach for his drink, casually turning in the direction Connie'd indicated. 'Them?'

'The boys under the beach towel. They aren't fucking but, by the movements, there's some very vigorous mutual masturbation going on.'

'How sweet. I imagine they'll be heading for the float soon, then.'

'The float?'

'See it? Anchored about a hundred yards offshore?'

'I see it.'

'It seems to be considered to be in international waters. There's no taboo on fucking and so on out there. When it started, people would swim out and hang onto the other side and get it on while invisible from the shore. Now it's become accepted. If you swim out there you take your chances on what you might see. People swim out there solo and hook up there if they meet anyone they fancy, or they swap. It's pretty much an ongoing orgy on that platform a lot of the time.'

'What a good idea, for those who are alone. How far away did you say it was?'

'About a hundred yards, or metres if you prefer.'

'I've swum that far.'

'In the sea or in a pool?'

'A pool.'

'Better not go alone, then, for safety's sake. There's a current and the waves can get choppy once you're away from the shore. If you wanted to try it I'd escort you and not interfere with what you did when you got there, if that's what you wanted.'

'You're kind, Rupert, but I don't think I'm up to diving naked into an orgy with a group of strangers, not yet. If *you* decide to check the action out, though, I'd like to come along. I wouldn't *have* to pass myself around, would I?'

'Not at all. Some people go out just to watch. Some go with partners because they want to *be* watched. It's very easy going, no pressure ever, not that I've heard of. What do you think?'

Connie took a breath. 'Sure, I'll try it. We can always turn around and come back if we like, right?'

'Of course.' He turned to Selena. 'Lovey, Connie would like to go take a look at whatever there is to be seen on the float. Want to come?'

Selena stretched up to peer out to sea. 'As far as I can see, there's no one there yet, but it's like when the band strikes up. Once the first couple start dancing, others follow. I'm ready when you are. We can get the ball rolling.' She stood, making the decision for the three of them.

Connie had her certificate for swimming ten lengths free-style, from her schooldays. That isn't quite the same as churning through the incoming Atlantic tide, as she soon found out. About halfway she began to get worried. Neither of her lovers were in sight. She stopped swimming and trod water.

'We're right here,' she heard Rupert call.

She looked towards the shore. The two of them were trailing her by about fifteen feet, a little to each side.

'We're watching out for you,' Selena reassured her. 'Are you OK or do you want to go back?'

That was so touching. They hadn't said anything that might have embarrassed her but they were looking after her like the good friends they'd so quickly become. Of course, if Jeff had been there, he'd have done the same. 'I'm fine,' she called back, 'but if you could keep an eye on me?'

'Of course. Brave girl,' Rupert told her.

Knowing that she had guardian angels seemed to put strength into Connie's arms and legs. The second fifty yards were easier than the first had been. Even so, she was panting when she was finally able to grab the edge of the float. Seconds later, big hands took hold of her ribcage and heaved her up onto the flat surface.

'Thanks,' she gasped.

'You're welcome.' Rupert sat up beside her.

Selena joined them. 'We seem to be early for the party,' she observed.

'I'm never early,' Rupert said. 'Everyone else must be late. Shall we start without them?'

'Make love, right here on top, where everyone can see us?' Connie mused. The thought wasn't uninviting.

'People bring binoculars to the beach for that very reason,' Rupert told her, 'but that'd be a bit ostentatious for the first arrivals, like the first dance at a ball being The Chicken Dance. Orgies need to warm up or else people get put off. No, Connie, not on the deck. I suggest we start discreetly. People will be intrigued and those who are into it will be drawn to join us.'

'Show me what you mean.'

'Of course.' Rupert stood up. He already had an erection big enough that Connie was sure the people on shore could see it. He waved towards the beach and dived in.

'He's so shy, poor man,' Connie remarked to Selena.

'Painful, isn't it.'

From the water, Rupert called, 'Hang off the raft, Connie. Just hold on to it and let yourself float on your back.'

She stepped off the deck and caught the edge as she fell.

Rupert told her, 'Turn your back to the deck and hold on above your head. Let your legs float up, spread wide, preferably.'

'Weightless fucking? That'll be a first for me.'

'Better than a waterbed, not as good as freefall, I imagine.'

'There's something you've never tried?'

'There always is, isn't there. That's the joy of it.'

Rupert trod water and sculled himself towards Connie, between her calves, her knees, her thighs, and bent forward to reach round and get a hand on her back. She felt him manoeuvring his cock, fumbling with it under the waves, and then it was tucked under her with her slit on the upper surface of his shaft.

'I'd prefer it inside me if it's all the same to you,' she told him.

'Picky, picky, picky.'

He manoeuvred some more. His knob found its way between her lips, and into her. 'I could just let the waves do all the work from here on,' he observed.

'No, it's not rough enough, Rupert. You are going to have to put some effort into it, I'm afraid.' She hitched and ground down to get some friction between her clit and his cock. It felt as if there was some seawater inside her, pushed in by his cock's entrance, but that couldn't hurt, could it? Might do her some good.

Selena said, 'Less witty repartee, more raw fucking, please.' Her face had appeared beside Connie's, dangling down from where she was sprawled on the deck above.

Connie turned her head to face her friend's reversed head. 'Upside-down kiss?'

'Love it.'

They extended tongues that met flat-on-flat in a way that is impossible to achieve in any other juxtaposition.

A clear tenor voice asked, 'Excuse us, but is it OK to watch you people? It's our first visit and we aren't sure of the etiquette.'

'How polite,' Rupert said. 'By all means. Anyone who comes to the platform is ready to be watched, at least. You're welcome to observe.'

Connie twisted to look up and back, dislodging Rupert's cock. Two young men had joined Selena on the platform, one on each side of her. They might have been the couple who'd been fondling under the beach towel. One was a platinum blond, with shoulder-length locks that would have been flowing if they hadn't been sodden. The other's hair was jet black, in an urchin cut that had almost dried out already. Both were romance-novel handsome – 'sweet' romance', not 'bad boy'.

The blond said, 'I'm Perry. This is Drew. Thanks for the invitation. People who like to watch can be misunderstood.'

'Not here,' Rupert assured him. He introduced Connie and Selena.

Connie curled up against Rupert so that she could whisper in his ear. 'Considering our audience, Rupert, do me up my bum. Let's make it worth their while to have swum all the way out here.'

138

He whispered back, 'That's very thoughtful of you, Connie. I agree, let's give them a show.' He took hold of the platform with both hands to let Connie twist around to face it. 'Let's try this,' he said. Holding on to the platform with one hand, he lifted Connie's thigh up with the other, taking her weight back across his body. He hooked that heel over the edge. 'Hold her steady, would you?' he asked.

Drew wrapped a hand around Connie's slender ankle.

Rupert lifted Connie's other leg for Perry to take hold of.

'Good job I'm flexible,' Connie remarked with a grunt.

'One of your more endearing characteristics,' he told her. 'Selena, perhaps you could steady our girl's arms for her?'

Connie looked up at the three expectant faces that were looking down at her. She had an *audience*! Watching their eyes, she told Rupert, 'Fuck my bottom, please, Rupert. Do me up my bum-hole. If it's tight, force it. Don't have any mercy on me.'

She felt him kiss her back, presumably in approval of her adding dialogue to their little scene. Well, from on the platform, they couldn't actually see what Rupert was doing to her underwater, so it was best she give them a blow-by-blow.

'I can feel you between my cheeks, Rupert. Don't wait. I want it. That's it, that's my hole. Press harder. I can take it. Yes ... Yes ... Yes ... I can feel myself opening up for you, Rupert. Force it in. I don't care how big it is or how tight I am, *make* me take it.

'Oh God, yes. That hurts *sooo* good! More, please. More. All the way in. You're so deep inside me, Rupert. Oh yes!'

Her commentary was cut short by Selena leaning further down and getting her mouth to Connie's. Through the avid wet kissing, Connie contributed by grunting with each of Rupert's thrusts. Selena pulled back but her hand behind Drew's neck pushed his face down to feast from Connie's mouth, and twisted her head to kiss Perry.

That was new! Connie had never, to the best of her knowledge, kissed a gay man before. Perhaps they weren't gay? No, had to be, on the gay side of bi, maybe. They'd most likely fuck women, then, once in a while.

The three observers, Perry, Selena and Drew, passed Connie's mouth from one to the other as well as kissing each other and ... yes, Perry and Drew were kissing now. Their kisses didn't look any different than boy-girl kisses, or girl-girl. How could they?

Selena's head withdrew. The boys took her place steadying Connie's arms. Perry pulled up a little – not abandoning her, she hoped. No, he'd decided to slaver her foot with kisses, sucking on her toes and slithering his tongue between them.

Drew said, 'That's nice, just like that!'

Connie asked, 'What?'

'Your friend, Selena. She's playing with us, back there. She's got her fingers up my bum and she's found my nut to massage.'

'She's a bitch,' Connie told him.

'Just like you!' He kissed her, groaning into her mouth. Rupert was buggering her with such fervour that he was frothing the water between them. Connie strained back at him and wriggled. When Drew pulled back from her mouth to suck a great gasp of air, she told Rupert, 'Come in my bum, you bastard! Give me your load. Come on, I want it so bad!'

And he did.

When he'd finished juddering, his fingers found her pussy and started exploring.

Connie whispered, 'It looks like being a long day, Rupert. I'd like to try some of that prolonged anticipation you talk about. Is that a problem for you?'

'By no means.' He helped her untangle herself and heaved her up onto the platform, scattering the other three.

Drew was first to climb to his hands and knees. 'That was great,' he said. 'You won't mind if I ...?' He nodded towards Perry.

'Go ahead,' Rupert told him. 'It's time we ate, if you won't feel abandoned. We're sure to see you around later.'

'That'd be nice.' He got to his lover and crawled over him. Mouths found cocks and suckled contentedly.

'In the water with us,' Rupert said. He dived in, followed by Selena.

Connie gave the boys a last lingering look and jumped in. When she bobbed to the surface, Rupert was waiting for her.

'I don't want you tiring yourself out,' he said. 'Turn on your back and relax.'

Connie rolled over. His hand took a hank of her hair, wrapped it around and started towing her by it.

'Does that hurt?' he called back to her.

The tugging did cause her some pain but whether it was because she hadn't climaxed from being buggered or because it was some primeval instinct, she found that she enjoyed it. 'I'm fine!' she shouted back. With nothing else to do while she was being towed, Connie indulged in a little caveman fantasy and diddled herself all the way back to the beach.

Chapter Sixteen

Selena and Rupert decided that they hadn't done enough about erasing their tan-lines, so they took Connie back to the beach the next day. She suspected that they, or at least Selena, didn't feel they were done with Drew and Perry.

Connie put the boys at about twenty. With their looks, they'd be targets for both cougars and fag-hags, not to mention leathermen, bears and any men who were just 'straight gay'. Connie was proud of her new vocabulary, picked up online during those lonely nights after she'd broken up with Jeff and before coming to the Dominican Republic.

What was Jeff doing these days? Maybe he and Shirley were a thing now, though she thought that Shirley was too good a friend to take advantage ...

It wouldn't be taking advantage, though, would it? She had no claim on Jeff any more. He could fuck whoever he wanted now, even fall in love, if he had that in him.

That thought was totally unfair. To get her mind off it, she put her day's costume together.

Her top was a cropped beige T-shirt in thin cotton that Tina had further cropped so that the hem now came down to exactly the tips of her nipples. Normal movement would have meant that her nipples were virtually on continuous display, but when she smeared Strip-Tack on her areolas, lifted her breast a little over an inch and pressed the shirt to her skin, she was left looking as if she was constantly about to pop a nipple out from under. That sort of support, as she'd already discovered, gave her a permanent slight uplift and enhanced the swing and sway of her breast.

The skirt looked like a pleated beige micro-skirt, very low-rise. The waistband buckled just below where the subtle crease above her pubes defined the gentle curve under her tummy. The pleats weren't real. They were individual strips of semi-stiffened fabric, attached to the waistband but not to each other, although they overlapped slightly. With every step she took, the strips swayed and exposed something – the tops of her thighs, her bottom and often her sex – but just for a fraction of a second at a time. It was about as daring a skirt as she could imagine getting away with. If there was anything of a wind … well, she'd deal with that if it happened.

She had beige espadrilles for her feet and a bush hat to shield her face.

Connie made a sex show out of getting into Rupert's golf cart, pausing for a count of three when halfway. The cart had no doors, so you had to step over the sides. It was ideal for showing off her skirt's potential, both from her point of view and from the passengers'.

'Lovely,' Selena told her.

'Thanks.'

'I'd love to see you do the hula in that.'

'Thanks for the inspiration.'

'I'd settle for watching you do a hula out of it,' Rupert said. 'Or the limbo.'

Selena, sandwiched between the others, rested one hand on the crotch of Rupert's pants and slid the other between the panels of Connie's skirt. 'You two!' she admonished. 'It's barely ten in the morning and you're both horny already.'

Connie twisted on her seat and gave her friend a long deep wet kiss. 'There, that's three of us.' Her fingers touched the black net pouch that cupped Selena's pubes and they came away damp. She held that aromatic hand up to Selena's lips. 'And don't you try to deny it.'

'I wouldn't dream of it!'

Laughing companionably, they drove to the beach parking area.

Rupert had brought a laptop with him to the beach. Selena had a stack of folders with papers in them that she had to go through. They both apologised for having to work.

145

Connie settled down with their binoculars, mainly hoping to detect someone secretly ogling her. The naked beach volleyball was fun to watch but the players were all her junior by a year or two so she felt excluded from that. Not that the eighteen- and nineteen-year-olds weren't attractive – they were – but doing any of them would have made her feel like a cougar and she wasn't ready for that role yet. Maybe when she reached Selena's age.

Drew and Perry didn't show up until after lunch. They waved at her and settled down under their giant beach towel. Connie had no problem imagining what was going on beneath it but she could hardly join them.

She was sure that if invited they'd swim out to the platform with her. If she did, though, Rupert would be bound by his protective instincts to accompany her. That wouldn't be fair.

The heat of the sun, she was finding, made her horny, particularly when it shone directly onto her newly bald pussy. It was very sunny. That wasn't likely to change before the evening.

What if she hid under something and diddled herself? No, Rupert or Selena would be bound to notice and insist on taking care of her needs. Damn! She could get dressed and head back to a pool or one of the bars and see what developed. Her outfit would get her plenty of attention. But Selena and Rupert might feel abandoned. She didn't expect them to amuse her twenty-four hours a day, seven days a week, but they wouldn't understand that. Sometimes friends can be too nice; it puts you under an obligation.

That was a nasty thought. She should think about sex, not relationships. That's always safe, and fun. At least, it was now that she'd reinvented herself – it hadn't used to be.

She should apply logical analysis. She had two gay boys she could use to amuse herself, she was sure, but only if she could manage it somewhere close by.

Of course!

Connie marched over to where the gay lads were hidden under their towel. It was good that she'd taken action. If they got off, they might not be so amenable. She toed the place where a bum bulged the towel. 'Perry? Drew?'

Their hot faces appeared.

'Follow me,' she said, and marched away. Of course, if they didn't follow her, her plan was a bust. After twenty paces she looked back. They were trailing her, awkwardly trying to hide the erections they'd given each other. Good.

Connie made for the row of showers and opened a frosted-glass door. As she'd been told, there was room for two, easily. Three should be able to manage if one was as slender as she was. She held the door open and ushered them inside before following and setting the lock to 'occupied'. It really was quite crowded, bare skin against bare skin.

'Turn it on, then,' she ordered.

Perry reached up to the controls. Pulsating jets came at them from two sides. Even the beach showers were upscale here.

'Let me get between you,' she asked, turning sideways and wriggling in. 'I've always wanted to do this,' she lied. She'd only just thought of it. 'But my straight men friends won't go for it. You two don't mind if I blow you both at once, do you?' Jets of water were thrumming on her breasts.

Perry said, 'Not at all.'

Drew added, 'Fine by me, Connie. Your friend Rupert doesn't swing both ways, then?'

'No, sorry.'

'Pity.'

She squatted, sliding down against their slippery, wet, muscular young bodies. As they were half-turned towards each other, their erections almost bumped heads at about the level of their navels. Both cocks were already wet, and not from the shower. Tiny bubbles of pre-cum dribbled down their undersides.

'Yummy,' she told them. The flow of water that ran off Drew's chest and the one from Perry's spattered the back of Connie's neck. She turned her face to catch some of it in her mouth and then squirted the mouthful onto the heads of their cocks.

'You don't mind if we make out some while you do that, do you?' asked Drew.

'Go for it, boys, but don't crush me between you, OK?'

They turned in towards each other for a passionate kiss. Connie wouldn't have minded watching but she'd declared her intentions and had better follow through. She took a shaft in each hand and began to pump slowly, being sure to hold their cocks so that their heads kept in slippery contact with each other.

Two cocks at once! She imagined that Selena would have tried that but most girls, Shirley, for example, would be both shocked and impressed. This was a tale she had to remember to recount to her real-life friend, when she got back to the office.

'Back to the office' was a dismal thought. Being an actuary paid well, but that was the best that could be said of it.

Perry was tweaking his lover's left nipple. Apart from the obvious, boy-boy loving wasn't that different from the heterosexual kind.

Connie managed to stretch her right hand around both of their shafts together, even though her fingertips didn't meet, and kept stroking as she pulled their heads into contact with the flat of her tongue. That left her free hand to caress their bodies. Being careful with her nails, she raked her hooked fingers across first one flat belly, then the other. Being less careful, she scratched four shallow grooves across Drew's bum, then down Perry's. Straight men liked to have scratch marks to show off.

Gays would likely be the same. They could kiss each other's scars better tomorrow, and think of her.

She'd promised them blow-jobs. Easier to say than do. She didn't have a big mouth and these two were pretty well hung, in her estimation. They weren't as big as Jeff, of course, but their cocks' heads were still pretty large.

To start, she laved their heads with her tongue, savouring the clear fluids that they leaked. Now if she just ... No, it wasn't going to work using one hand. She got their cocks between her two palms and squeezed as much as she dared. Cocks' heads, unlike balls, are tough, but they aren't indestructible. With the heads squished together, she worked them into her mouth from the corner, pushing Perry's part-way into her cheek and stretching to get as much of Drew's into the other side of her mouth as she could accommodate. Yes, both were past her lips. That was quite an achievement. But that was as far in as they were going to go, both together. Mouths can stretch, but within limits. She could lavish attention on both heads with her tongue but pumping both at once with her mouth was out of the question.

She'd just do the best she could.

Connie started over with one shaft in each fist. Her mouth bobbed on Drew's as her hand worked on Perry's, then she switched. Judging by the boys' groans and the way they were pawing each other, they were enjoying her ministrations. Would she be able to get them off that way, if she kept going? Likely, yes.

Years ago, long before she'd discarded her modesty, she'd had a dream that she'd tried hard to forget, of her being naked with dozens of male lovers, in all shapes and sizes. The dream had been both confused and confusing and her suppression of it had been partially successful, but the main lingering trace was that she'd been able to bring those men to climaxes four, five and six at a time. Just how she'd achieved that was lost in the mists of memory.

Now she had two cocks to service, for real. And, she realised, two at a time was enough. With two, she could retain some degree of control.

As if to deny her thoughts, she felt a fist knot in her hair and the cock she had in her mouth pushed in a little deeper.

Another hand grabbed her hair from the other side. Her head was twisted, not violently but firmly, off the first cock and directed to the second one, which was eagerly pushing at her lips. No sooner had she given *that* cock a good strong suck than her head was pulled back to the first.

She was safe. Of course she was. These were good, civilised boys, not thugs or rapists. It was fine that she felt a little nervous thrill. That can be a positive part of sex, with people you trust. Still, it was time she took charge again.

Holding both of their cocks as if they were handles, Connie pushed up into the water's jets, ignoring the directions the hands were trying to move her head in. When she tried to stand, Drew and Perry released her hair instantly.

'You OK, Connie?' Perry asked.

'We weren't too rough on you?' Drew added.

'I'm fine, boys. Nice cocks.'

'Thanks.'

'How about you fuck me now? Both at once? Drew, you want to take the back way in while Perry does me in my pussy?'

Drew nodded eagerly. Perry showed no reaction.

'It doesn't have teeth, Perry,' she assured him. 'Try it. You might like it.'

'It's not that.' He looked at his lover. 'You don't mind, Drew?'

Obviously there was a subtext going on that Connie didn't know about. 'I won't turn him straight, Drew, I promise. It'd just be for fun, a one-time thing. If you have a problem with it, forget it. No hard feelings.' Oh God, this was unreal. Here she was, trying to talk a couple of lusty young gay men into fucking and buggering her when just about every healthy and straight man in the world would have jumped at the chance to do either to her. And she'd already had both of their cocks in her mouth.

Poor men. Being the pursuer wasn't much fun. She'd take being seduced over being the seducer any day. The one thing that the few, very few, men who had been successful in getting Connie into their beds had in common was confidence. A take-charge attitude worked wonders, provided it wasn't threatening. OK. She could do that.

Connie looked Perry straight in his eyes. She put the flat of her hand on his muscular chest and pushed him back against the glass wall. 'Bend your legs a bit, Perry,' she ordered. 'Get it down where it'll be useful.' She tugged down on his cock to reinforce her words. 'Bum off the glass, please?'

Perry's upper back slithered down wet glass with a squeak.

'Good. Hold it right there.' She twisted her head. 'Drew, brace me from behind, OK?'

He wrapped his arms around her chest and pulled her back against his chest. Connie lifted herself up and wrapped her legs around Perry's thighs. Gripping hard with her legs, she said, 'Put it in me, please, Perry, or do you want Drew to do it for us?'

He looked dubious but he told her, 'I can do it, Connie.'

Even so, she reached down between them to give him a quick encouraging stroke. His hand took over from her. His cock's head nudged at her slit uncertainly. She took over again, and pushed him inside her, just his head.

Felix Baron

'Thanks.'

'You're welcome.' Over her shoulder she said, 'Drew, can you find your way into my bum-hole?'

'Sure can, Connie,' he assured her.

Connie smiled. She was all for sex being fun but this was getting farcical.

With what felt like a very assured hand, Drew introduced his cock to Connie's sphincter. 'Ready?'

'Can you both go in at once?' she asked. 'That's part of my fantasy.'

'Fulfilling fantasies is what we're all about,' Drew told her. 'Ready, Perry?'

Perry nodded.

Connie translated, 'He's ready when you are, Drew.'

As one, two stiff cocks surged into her and up. It was so *filling*. Somehow, it felt more loving than invasive, not that those are incompatible. Connie felt engorged. Her insides seemed to be moved aside, rearranged to allow her to accommodate all the delicious man-flesh that was invading her. She surrendered happily.

'That's so nice,' she purred. 'Do me, both of you. Enjoy!'

They started to pump. Perry seemed to have abandoned his doubts. The expression on his face was one of pure bliss. Both of the boys worked their hips, rotating and grinding.

'Can you feel Drew's cock, Perry?' she asked.

154

'Hm.'

'Can you feel Perry's, Drew?'

'Oh yes.'

'Feel good?'

They both said, 'Yes.'

'Then go for it. Don't worry about me. Just use me, please. Fuck each other through me, that's what I want.'

Their deep thrusts became more urgent. Drew bit into Connie's left shoulder. It felt as if he'd leave a bruise but she didn't care. Perry sank his teeth, not too hard, into her right shoulder. They both jolted into her.

'That's so nice,' she told them. 'It feels good, having both of you inside me at once. This is my first time doing this, did you know?'

They ignored her question.

'You always remember your firsts, don't you. I do. First kiss. First grope. First time I gave a boy a hand-job – blow-job, too. First fuck. Now, my first double with my first gays. I'll keep you in my memory for ever, Drew, Perry.'

Perry was good enough to say, 'That's nice.'

Connie was being jolted, held up by the two cocks inside her. The shaking made it impossible for her to talk coherently but that didn't matter. She wasn't going to come. The boys didn't know or didn't care enough to work her clit for her and she couldn't be bothered to do it for herself. It was all about new sensations, not at all about getting off.

They were panting now, and heaving her up and down like she was cork afloat on a stormy sea.

Drew made a peculiar grating noise in Connie's ear, followed by a series of deep grunts.

Perry said, 'Yes, yes, yes!'

Connie's upper body was pushed aside, not roughly, so that the two boys could get their faces together for a deep wet kiss.

And there was wet inside Connie, as well. She could feel it in her pussy and guessed that it was wet inside her rectum too. The boys sighed and lowered her to her feet. She untangled herself. As she splashed cupped palms of water at her sex and bottom, she told them, 'That was very nice, thank you, boys. If you'll excuse me, I'll leave first. Some people might raise their eyebrows if we all left at once.'

'Not here,' Perry said.

'Even so.'

On leaving the shower, Connie wandered down to the beach instead of heading straight back to Selena and Rupert. She waded into the water and out, without swimming, until the cleansing Atlantic Ocean washed over her shoulders. Standing there, pretty well invisible from the shore, she fingered herself into a nice little underwater orgasm.

The face in her mind at her moment of climax was Jeff's.

Chapter Seventeen

On Friday, Connie, Selena and Rupert spent the afternoon at The Juke Joint, which was all green Naugahyde,
chrome and neon. Fifties music played. The servers, all
busty blonde girls, wore poodle skirts that were anach-
ronistically short and tight angora sweaters. The only
things on the menu were burgers, fries and onion rings,
but there were fifty different burgers. The plates were
the size of platters, and overflowed. To drink, there was
a variety of brands of pop and fifteen flavours of milk
shakes, all of which you ordered 'with' or 'without'.
'With' meant that they were laced with white rum.

Rupert and Selena jived, and performed well, as far as
Connie could judge. She'd never danced – never been to
a dance hall or at a wedding where there was dancing,
or even music. It was fun watching her friends perform.
Perhaps she could take lessons some time. She'd heard it
said that good dancers make good lovers. Maybe that's
why her mother and her sect were so against dancing.

Felix Baron

Rupert leaned towards Connie with an uncharacteristi-
cally serious expression on his face. 'Connie, could you
possibly do us an enormous favour?'

'Of course. Anything.'

'Never say you'll do "anything", it can get you into
trouble,' he advised. 'Tomorrow evening, Selena and I
are entertaining for dinner. Our guests – Angus and his
wife – and Selena and I might be getting into something
together. We'll be feeling him and his wife out, as it were.'

'Feeling out?' she asked pertly.

'No, silly. Not that. Strictly business. He's in his seven-
ties and his wife, Dolly, is at least sixty-five.'

'But not dead yet?'

'Seriously, Connie, this is nothing directly to do with
sex. If you can come, I'd like you to dress conservatively.
Prettily, of course, but no deep cleavage or flashing thighs,
not even a hint. Can do?'

'No problem.' She had all the party clothes she'd
packed, none of which had been worn.

'The reason I want you along,' he explained, 'is that
they are bringing a friend, of sorts, whom I'd like you
to entertain for me.'

Connie sat back. Was he setting her up? Was she
supposed to repay all their kindnesses by 'entertaining'
their superfluous guest?

Rupert continued. 'Let me explain this right, so there
are no misunderstandings. Our extra guest, named Doreen,

158

I believe, is their toy-girl. She's paid as a companion and, I suspect, to fuck them, either one or both, I'm not sure. I know that she's been with them for almost a year.'

'She's a prostitute.'

'Not exactly. There's a hierarchy in these things. Where "paid to be in a ménage" ranks compared to "professional escort" I'm not sure, but girls like her don't come cheap. She's about your age. Selena and I want to talk business to Angus and Dolly. All I ask of you is that you make nice and keep Doreen occupied.'

'But not sexually?'

'Not sexually; socially.'

'I can do that. I'd be glad to.'

'You're an angel. Eight o'clock? Our place? I'll send a driver for you at about quarter to?'

'I'll be able, willing, and ready, as always, but "not sexually".'

* * *

Angus was short, portly, bald and wore an immaculate little white beard. Dolly had a blue rinse and makeup that didn't try to conceal her age. Connie took an instant liking to them both, particularly to Angus's accent.

Doreen had honey-blonde hair done in a bob and vulpine features with a slight overbite. She would have been showing more cleavage than Connie if she'd had what it takes to make a cleavage. She wasn't unattractive

159

but was certainly nothing spectacular. If she was near the top of her chosen profession, she had to be very good at something or another.

Dinner was catered by Chez Aphrodite. That was fine by Connie. She was far from being bored with shellfish yet. During the meal, Selena and Rupert and Angus and Dolly talked politics and economics. Both were topics that interested Connie but she listened dutifully and confined her contributions to nods and smiles. As the meal was being cleared away, Rupert led his guests to where four armchairs surrounded a low table. There were notepads and pens. Time for Connie to do her stuff. Doreen had been drinking gin and tonics with lemon twists, so Connie mixed two.

'Have you seen their Japanese garden?' she asked Doreen.

'No, I haven't.'

'Would you like to?'

'Sure.'

There was a bench seat near the small pond. Connie made for it. She was just in time to call, 'This way, Doreen,' before the girl put her foot down on a bed of carefully raked sand.

Doreen joined her. Connie tried to talk fashion, though she only knew what was sexy, not what was in style. Doreen didn't seem interested. Who would win Oscars didn't engage her either. When it came to TV, she knew the shopping channels well but never watched comedy or drama. An uncomfortable silence fell.

At last, Doreen spoke first. 'Want to go upstairs and make out?' she asked Connie.

It would have been a lot less strain than making conversation with this girl, but Connie politely declined.

'They got you on an exclusive deal, do they?' Doreen asked.

Oh damn! This idiot obviously thought that she had the same arrangement with Rupert and Selena that she herself had with Angus and Dolly. Connie said, 'They had me sign an NDA – non-disclosure agreement,' she lied.

'I can dig it. So, have you tried that new lube, "Play-O"?'

'No. Is it any good?' At last, they had something in common to talk about!

When the guests finally left, around ten-thirty because Angus didn't like to stay up too late, Rupert handed Connie an envelope.

'What's this?' she asked.

'You were great tonight, but it was no fun for you at all. I want to pay you for your time.'

She handed it back. 'Don't you dare.'

'Thank you.' He paused. 'Connie, it went very well between them and us tonight. The bad news is, as a result, Selena and I have to head back home tomorrow.'

'Oh.'

'We'll try to get back here before your vacation is over but this might be goodbye for a little while.'

'Oh.' She'd been avoiding thinking about it, but the end had to come. She'd known that. She'd also ignored it. 'I'm glad that your business talks went well.'

'If we don't get back in time to see you before you leave, we'll get in touch later, Connie.'

Numbly, she said, 'That'd be nice.'

She left their home without another word. Oh well. She'd have memories. How could she have thought there'd be more? She should have taken his damned money.

* * *

When she got back to her suite, there was a note waiting. It was Tina, just her name and phone number. It was eleven but it looked like the woman would be waiting up for her.

'Hi!' Tina said. 'Thanks for calling. I was wondering what time you planned for us to get together tomorrow.'

Damn! She'd forgotten her promise. 'How about ten? No, make that eleven. OK for you?'

'I'll be there. I've been looking forward to it.'

So had Connie, for the first couple of days. Then she'd got so wrapped up in having a good time that she'd forgotten the woman who'd made her good times possible. She didn't deserve real friends. She'd doted on

Rupert and Selena, big-shot executives, who just wanted to use her, while ignoring the less glamorous boutique manager who only wanted to be her friend – with benefits, of course.

Not feeling at all good about herself, Connie went to bed and had a nice little cry.

Chapter Eighteen

There was someone knocking at the door. Connie aimed an eye at the clock. When it swam into focus it told her it was eleven-oh-two.

Tina!

Connie scrambled out of bed, called, 'I'm coming,' grabbed a robe and stumbled to the door. The woman outside was blonde, with flip-ups. She was wearing glossy black knee boots with five-inch heels and a matching vinyl raincoat that barely reached her naked thighs. An overnight bag sat on the floor at her feet.

Connie peered. 'Tina?'

'Did you tie one on last night?'

'No, not, not at all.'

'You want me to come back later?'

'No. Sorry. I slept in.'

'Really?'

'Come on in, Tina. Forgive me. I didn't recognise you at first.'

'A wig can do that.'

'Yes it can, it seems.'

Connie set the machine to making coffee. 'Those outfits that you altered for me, Tina, I have to thank you. Boy, do they work.'

'So you've been mobbed by guys?'

'Not exactly mobbed but I certainly got all the attention I could handle.'

'Just men, or women as well?' There was a trace of jealousy in her voice.

'Men for the most part, including a couple of gays.'

'You a fag-hag?'

'Aren't we all, to some extent?' She poured. 'How do you like your coffee?'

'Black, but I like you just the way you are.' Her voice lilted.

It took Connie a moment to make the connection. 'The way I am, right now, is in dire need of a shower. Give me ten?'

'Need a hand?'

'Let me wake up first.' If she'd had any doubts, she lost them. Tina had come expecting sex. How did she feel about that? Just fine. If you fall off a horse ... Or a pair of horses, come to that.

Fifteen minutes later, Connie was back, dewy, in a fresh robe. She'd managed to dab on some lips and eyes. 'Did you have anywhere in mind for us to go, or do?' she asked.

'I thought that we could just hang out.'

'Why don't you take your coat off, then? Is it raining out?'

'No rain. No clouds. Just another boring perfect day.' Tina unbelted her coat and tossed it across a chair. That left her in nothing but her boots. She posed, hipshot.

'Wow!' Connie said.

Tina looked unsure. 'Did I read the signals wrong?' she asked.

Connie shed her robe. 'Not at all.' A thought struck her. 'Minute.' She took the Do Not Disturb sign from the credenza, hid behind the door as she opened it, and hooked it over the knob. 'That's better.' When she turned around, Tina was tucking the bedclothes up under her chin. Her boots were in the corner, Connie was pleased to note.

She strode to the bed, whipped the bedclothes off and tossed them to the floor. 'I prefer it this way,' she declared. She looked around the room. 'No, not quite.' There was a dressing table opposite the foot of the bed. She went to it and tilted the mirror. 'Tell me when you can see yourself, please,' she asked Tina.

'More that way. Wait. Another inch of tilt. Perfect – provided we don't move around too much.'

'I plan to move around a lot, but nothing's perfect, except maybe for your body. Tina, you're *gorgeous*.'

'After all the naked bodies you've seen this week?'

'After, or before. Or during. You'd stand up to *any* comparison. Let me get a good look at you!'

A little bit of exaggeration never does any harm when it comes to paying compliments but Tina really was lovely. Her breasts were about the same size as Connie's, but stood out a bit more, like she'd been doing some special uplifting exercises. Her waist looked an inch trimmer and her hips another inch more curvaceous. Her navel could have held one of those belly-dancers' jewels. Tina's sex was as smooth as Connie's, but its lips pouted a little, making it look a tad more mature – or less immature? Connie didn't have to force the appreciation into her eyes.

'You'll make me blush,' Tina said, 'looking at me like that. And you're the one who had problems with being too modest?'

'I think I've overcome that particular character flaw.'

'Good. How about your other flaws?'

'Such as?'

'Such as being a horny little bitch with the morals of a minx in heat?'

There was only one appropriate response to that. Connie took a dive onto the bed and landed with her face a few inches above the gentle curve of Tina's belly, just below her navel. Her lips descended. She blew a wet raspberry, the kind that mothers have been blowing on their infants' tummies since we fell out of the trees. Tina convulsed with giggles. Connie blew again.

Tina managed, 'Stop! Either stop or do it lower!'

It occurred to Connie that through all her wild sexual adventures of the past few days, she hadn't once performed orally on a woman, not counting once drinking champagne from Selena's pussy, which wasn't really the same.

She blew a raspberry on Tina's mound. The woman's hands flattened on the top of Connie's head, gently urging it lower.

'Here?' Connie asked, and blew a raspberry into the crease of Tina's right groin.

'Downnnn!' Tina pleaded.

'Here?' That one into the left crease.

'If you don't do it, I'll go crazy, Connie. I've thought of nothing else all week.'

'How about ...' Connie managed to work her head way down between Tina's thighs, past her sex, and get her lips on that sweet spot between pussy and anus. She blew again.

Tina went berserk with squirming laughter. Connie kept blowing until Tina's hilarity started to sound desperate. She'd just decided to cut the teasing when the slender thighs she'd had her head between clamped tight on her face. With a mighty heave, Tina rolled over, forcing Connie to do the same. They ended up with Tina sitting on Connie's mouth.

'*Now* do it,' Tina ordered.

'I give up, I give up,' Connie panted between the wet lips of Tina's pussy.

'You have to pay a forfeit,' Tina told her.

'What forfeit?'

'Sex slave?'

'Who being whose?'

'You, mine.'

'For how long?'

'Until I've come – twice.'

''K.'

'Say, "Yes, Mistress Tina, O mighty warrior Princess."'

'Yes, Mistress Tina, O mighty warrior Princess.'

'That's better.'

Being Tina's play-slave was very handy. It'd conceal her lack of experience when it came to giving oral sex to females. In any case, you can't go wrong following instructions if you listen carefully.

Tina hitched forward to fully cover Connie's mouth with the splayed lips of her sex.

With each breath that Connie took, she inhaled her friend's intimate aroma. Pheromones are addictive. She'd got hooked on Selena's and Rupert's. The best cure would be to replace her dependence on their pheromones with one on Tina's. She might end up a Tina-junkie, but she'd face that problem when and if it arose.

Tina commanded, 'Make a long tongue now, slave. Push it in deep. Good slave. Wag it. Lap it. Rotate, all the way round. That's it, explore me. Eat me all up.'

Connie did her best to comply, working at it so hard that the roots of her tongue ached.

Tina hitched forward more so that the lips of her pussy engulfed Connie's chin. 'My bum-hole next, slave. See how deep inside it you can get that nasty tongue of yours.'

Without hesitating, Connie complied. Tina ground down on Connie's chin as if she was trying to force her entire head into her body. Connie felt Tina's fingers on her nipples, rotating and plucking. The little nubs engorged until they felt like hard rubber. Tina moved again, arching over. Connie felt a kiss on her navel, then a tongue tip swirling inside. She had to strain her neck up to keep her tongue's contact with her 'Princess's little knot. Then she lost contact as Tina's licks worked lower, all the way down to the parted lips of Connie's pussy.

Tina rolled them onto their sides, mouths to pussies, classic sixty-nine, and devoured Connie, giving her no further instructions, just letting her lick and suck and nibble at will. Connie came first but she didn't slow her attentions down. She was a slave until Tina had climaxed twice, and she was eager to work off her indentureship.

Tina grunted and rolled aside.

'One?' Connie asked.

'No, just break time.'

'You're kidding!'

'Princesses don't kid. Feel for yourself.'

Connie felt Tina's pussy, though she couldn't be sure from that whether she had climaxed or not. The woman was very damp, but she'd been thoroughly licked for a long time. In any case, a woman can get wet without it meaning she's been satisfied.

'Sit up on the end of the bed facing the mirror,' Tina ordered.

She retrieved her bag and took out two foot-long submarine sandwiches and a bottle of 150 proof local rum. 'I brought lunch, just in case,' she explained. 'Pop in the minibar?'

'Help yourself.'

'Thanks.'

They sat watching themselves and each other as they devoured their sandwiches and washed them down with powerful Cuba Libres. Tina ate with her right hand and Connie with her left. Their free hands rested in each other's lap, fondling idly. For Connie, it was breakfast despite it being past noon. That made the meal suitably decadent. Almost by reflex, she asked herself what her mother would have said if she'd ever seen Connie like this. To her surprise, the question carried no emotional charge whatsoever, not even defiance. She just didn't care if what she did would have shocked her mother or not.

Did that mean that she was finally completely free?

She hooked a finger into Tina's pussy to find her clit. Half of her sandwich was gone. She set it aside and swigged the rest of her drink. 'Would you like some more of my tongue in you while you finish your sub?' she asked.

'Save this for later,' Tina replied. 'We look good in the mirror.'

'Yes, we do.'

'What depraved little bitches we are.'

'Yes, Princess, I cannot but agree.'

'Hold on.' Tina stretched back up the bed and tugged all the pillows and bolsters down to make a pile behind their backs. She jumped up and fetched a couple of chairs to set between their feet and the mirror. 'Like this!' She leaned back against the pillows and spread her legs wide, hooking her left thigh over Connie's right and resting her right heel up on a chair. 'Can you see my pussy OK?' she asked.

'Lovely.'

'Then let's diddle ourselves and watch each other, shall we?'

'Your word is my command, Princess.'

'Oops. I was forgetting something.' She jumped up and went back to her bag to return with a long white instrument, which she plugged into an outlet under the mirror. The shaft was about fourteen inches long. It had a short neck and then a white ball that was a bit smaller than a tennis ball. 'My Hitachi Magic Wand,' she explained. 'Are you familiar with it?'

'Is it a vibrator?'

'Yes.'

'I thought they looked like plastic cocks.'

'They can look like anything you could imagine and a few you can't, but this is my favourite. You should get one. It's good for girls and also for boys. If you are ever in a rush, the old Magic Wand can't be beat.'

'Really?'

'I'll let you try for yourself later. Meanwhile, my slave will perform for her Princess. Watch us in the mirror while we play with ourselves, OK?'

'OK.'

They slumped back against their pillows with their heads propped up to see the mirror. Connie was eager to see how Tina masturbated. For herself, she just rubbed around her clit but there had to be other ways to get off than by rubbing or by being licked.

Tina was rolling the ball of her thumb against the top of her index finger. Her clit had to be between the two. Connie copied. It felt nice, but not that different.

Tina grinned at her in the mirror. 'Feeling good?'

'Me? I'm just the tiniest bit nicely tipsy. I'm alone with the most beautiful woman in the entire damn Caribbean. The temperature is perfect and I have the rest of the day, a day filled with sweet kisses and intense orgasms, to look forward to. I am totally liberated, with not the slightest trace of guilt. I think that's about as good as it gets, Tina.'

'Back at ya!' The woman's fingers were masturbating

her clit in its sheath as if it was a tiny cock. Yeah – that felt good. Jeff had done her like that once or twice, as she remembered. She'd have liked him to do it that way more often but that had been back in the days when she was too shy to ask for what she wanted.

Jeff? Best not to think about him. No need to sour such a sweet day.

'Tina,' she asked, 'how many different ways do you use to diddle yourself?'

'Apart from with men or toys? By my own hands, as it were?'

'Yes.'

'Well …' She reached out sideways and retrieved a vial.

'Play-O?' Connie asked, proud to show off her recently acquired knowledge.

'No, just regular lube.' Tina poured some onto her right hand. 'OK, a manual on manual, by Tina the Terrible.'

'What happened to the warrior princess?'

'She's around here somewhere.' She turned her thighs outward and slathered the lube all over her pussy. When it was saturated, she cupped her hand over her sex, its heel on her mound, and rubbed, pushing down hard, in a circular motion.

Without taking her eyes off what her friend was doing, Connie groped for the lube and squirted a generous measure over her own pussy.

'Nice, huh?' Tina asked.

Connie nodded.

'Then there's like this ...' She pressed down on her lower tummy with her left hand and slapped her right palm down across herself, gentle little blows to start with, then harder and faster into a blurring erotic staccato.

Connie copied. It didn't hurt and it felt rather nice.

'Or ...' Tina continued. She gripped her clit's shaft between the first two knuckles of her hooked fingers and stabbed up and down in a curving motion so that she was finger-fucking herself at the same time as she frigged her clit. 'Oh. Nice. Hm, this is good, Connie. How is it for you?'

Connie managed, 'Mmmm.'

'But before we get off,' Tina said, 'it's time to introduce you to my Magic Wand.' She turned sideways towards Connie with the giant vibrator in her hand. 'Keep fingering yourself.'

The gadget hummed, low in pitch then higher. 'Two speeds, see?' Tina said. 'I always start on low power because it can feel too strong if you start with it full on.'

Connie nodded.

Tina ran the head of the device slowly and gently up the inside of Connie's right thigh. The buzzing-tingling felt delicious where the ball was in contact with her skin, but also around, below and above. The top nestled below Connie's pussy, sending little thrills into her bum and making the lips of her sex quiver.

'Nice?'

'Lovely.'

Tina rolled closer, to get her face close to Connie's pussy. The vibrator brushed against the lower half of Connie's left lip. She shivered.

'Good, huh?' Tina asked.

The head progressed up the length of one lip, avoided Connie's clit and ran down the other side. And again. Connie's thighs flexed of their own accord. The head rotated, teasing her lips apart. Tina moved it higher, onto the flat hard plane that covered Connie's pubic bone. She applied pressure. The bone itself vibrated. The Wand paused in the one spot while Tina fiddled with something. The hum rose in pitch until the quivering in Connie's flesh became almost electric.

'Like a climax?' Tina asked.

Connie nodded.

Her friend spat right on the exposed head of her clit. The fingers of her free hand folded the left lip of Connie's pussy over her clit. The vibrating rubber ball descended.

'Awwwww!' Connie convulsed. She curled up. The sensations were so exquisite that they were unbearable. She rolled away from Tina clutching herself protectively.

'What do you think?' her friend asked.

When she could speak, Connie asked, 'Can I do you with it?'

Tina dropped back, spread-eagled. 'What are you waiting for?'

* * *

When the subs were gone, they snacked on smoked almonds, Hickory Stix and jelly beans. Between making love, Connie put on a fashion show for Tina. Tina found a Latin American music channel on the TV and taught Connie some basic moves. A naked lambada led to more sex. At ten, Tina announced that she had to go. Off-duty staff were supposed to be gone by eleven.

'Next Sunday?' Connie asked. 'It'll be our last chance.'

'Sorry. Didn't I tell you? My company is transferring me. It's a new position and I'm not sure what I'll be doing but it's a big raise in pay.'

'So you're leaving?'

''Fraid so.'

'Well, goodbye then.' Connie retreated to the bathroom and ignored Tina's soft knocks until she heard the suite door close.

Over the course of the rest of her vacation Connie got involved with a swingers' club, four men and two other women, then had sex with a honeymoon couple and finally fucked Sten, who, it turned out, was a virgin.

She didn't make love to anyone.

Chapter Nineteen

On Connie's first day back at the office, Shirley greeted her with 'What a tan!'

'And no tan-lines,' Connie boasted.

'I don't believe you. Prove it!'

'Maybe I will.'

'When?'

'Give me a chance to get back into routine. Friday?'

Shirley seemed disappointed at having to wait but she accepted the invitation. Connie wanted the chance to get one of those Wands and some lube before she got it on with her friend for the first time. That's what would happen on Friday, she knew. Not so long before, Shirley had been Connie's guru. Connie had felt proud just to be seen with her. Now, the roles were reversed. It was Connie who was the sexual sophisticate. If Shirley proved a boring sex partner, a Wand and some lube would bring the evening to a happy and speedy climax, for Shirley at least.

When Connie opened Thursday's mail she started with her Visa bill. She owed twenty-eight dollars and twelve cents. How could it be so low? All the money she'd spent in Tina's Boutique? The next envelope contained a bill from that very boutique, for almost ten thousand dollars, marked PAID IN FULL – CASH. That was weird. Who ...?

The third envelope held nothing but a business card: Rupert Trevelian, no address, just a 1-800 number. She'd only ever met one Rupert. Connie dialled.

'Connie! Wonderful to hear from you. Unpacked yet?'

The bastard! He was carrying on just as if he'd never dumped her.

But had he?

He'd said he'd be in touch. She'd taken it as a sugar-coat for the brush-off. Now, it looked like he'd meant it. She'd put the worst interpretation on it. Connie, you are your own worst enemy.

She said, 'All unpacked. Tan fading. Missing the Island life and all its perks already. You two?'

'Busy, busy, busy. You free this weekend? Selena and I have a business proposition for you.'

'I'm free, but where? I have no idea where you are based. I'm not coming to Hong Kong for a day, if that's where you are.'

'How about St George's Tavern, on Emerald Street?'

'*My* Emerald Street?'

'Of course. Didn't you know that we're practically neighbours? You didn't Google us? We wouldn't have got so close to you if we'd had to say a permanent goodbye after your vacation. That would have been cruel, for all of us.'

'Yes, it would have. I should have guessed. Business proposition? What kind?'

'We'll explain when we see you, promise.'

'OK. One o'clock?'

'Good by us. Till then.'

Connie's date with Shirley didn't go exactly as she'd expected, but nothing ever did. Her friend proved very eager to inspect Connie's body and even gave it a few admiring and affectionate strokes but she seemed to take the most pleasure from Connie parading for her in her Tina-ised outfits and then letting Shirley try them on. She babbled about what whoever would say if they could see her now, with this or that part showing or next to. Like Connie, her greatest joy was in being looked at.

'If only we could go to work dressed like this,' she said.

'I don't think it'd suit everyone. Mrs Carrie, for instance. Her thighs …?'

'Not if everyone in the office dressed like this, silly. Just you and me.'

'And our jobs would be to drive everyone wild with desire, huh?'

'My kind of job,' Shirley confirmed.

'Be nice work,' Connie agreed.

Even when the two of them finally tumbled into Connie's bed to consummate their celebration of exhibitionism, Shirley mused, 'I wonder what your Jeff would think if he could see us two now, huh? I bet he's fantasised it.'

Connie stopped her silly chatter with a voracious kiss.

Chapter Twenty

Rupert was wearing a dark business suit. Selena, to Connie's amusement, had on a twin-set and pearls, just like Connie used to wear, but the skirt was tapered ankle-long and restricted her steps to a few short inches. Connie realised that covering up can be sexy, too.

Her own outfit was the business suit she'd bought way back when, against Shirley's advice, and had never before found an occasion to wear.

Rupert had whitebait, which Connie declined to try, or even look at, and a wedge of game pie, which also didn't appeal to her. She and Selena settled for bangers and mash.

'So what's this business proposition?' she asked over coffee. 'I hope you aren't selling Avon or looking for investors in a pyramid scheme.'

'Neither,' Selena assured her. 'You'll find it interesting, I think.'

'We'll show you.' Rupert pushed away from the table and dropped some bills on it.

He drove them out to the suburbs in his late-model Jag. They pulled up in front of a small block of apartments. 'Come on in!'

Connie trailed Rupert and Selena into the lobby.

'Twenty-four units, all being redone completely,' Rupert said. He stepped over a bundle of cables. 'Let's show you the top floor. That's pretty well finished.'

Connie remained silent and confused on the way up. There were two apartments on each floor. The one they showed her still smelled of the off-white paint. It was spacious, for a two-bedroom, with high ceilings and lots of natural light.

'What do you think?' Selena asked her. 'Could you see yourself comfortable in here?'

Connie narrowed her eyes. 'Are these for sale? Are you trying to sell me an apartment?'

'Of course not,' Rupert said.

'Rent me one?'

'No. Nothing like that,' he assured her. 'The deal we're offering is rent-free, no utilities, cable, air, everything, all for nothing if you decided to move here.'

What was a polite word? Connie asked, 'So you're opening a bordello?'

Both of her friends laughed.

'Hardly,' Selena told her. 'You like to show yourself off? We run a webcam business. We're offering you a part in it. You'd get paid, well, just for letting people look at you.'

That sounded strange, but interesting. 'I don't understand,' she said.

'A demonstration,' Rupert told her. He switched on a big flat TV. The picture resolved into a slightly overweight girl, naked, lying on a rumpled bed. She was chewing gum and filing her nails. The soles of her feet were filthy.

'Yeah, Dirty Jack Flesh,' the girl said. 'I get it. You'd like me to do the nasty to your wife while you watched, right?' She nodded. 'Never happen.'

'Is *that* what you want me to do?' Connie asked.

'That's the competition. Their girls do it strictly for the money. They have no standards. Even so, their girls are making an average of over three thousand a week each, part-time.'

'That's more than I make,' Connie said.

'In half the hours.'

'Why don't they work more?'

'Too lazy. Let me explain how it works in our operation. The customers go online, where they get a menu. It'll list all the girls, with pictures, and describe their personalities. There's also a menu of who will be working, and when, and what sort of things they'll be doing.'

'Such as?' Connie asked.

'Getting buggered,' Selena said. 'In one case, a girl we've got who is a contortionist, eating herself. Our punters can book time in advance according to what they fancy. They pay by the minute, two different rates, via a

900 number. At the standard rate, they get to watch and to hear the girl. Preferred rate, they can type messages and get into conversations with the girls, a limit of four doing that at any one time, to keep it manageable. *Our* way of working, we only partner with girls who are avid exhibitionists, so they enjoy what they do. We pick them for looks and we outfit them, costumes and wigs, so they can appear as two or more different girls. We have our own make-up artist to help out.'

'How long have you been open for business?'

'Two weeks, with four girls, so far.'

'What are *your* girls making?'

'Between six and ten thousand a week, working thirty-plus hours. Those girls already have their regulars, so that'll go up as they get more. We encourage our girls to lure customers back, with promises about what they'll be doing next Tuesday, at seven, for example. That works well. Some girls are developing online friendships, but they never meet their clients. In any case, this is the Web. We service the world. Out best customer so far lives in Hanoi. None of them know where we are, not even which country we are in, and we block out all calls within a five-hundred-mile radius, so you aren't going to bump into anyone at the supermarket, not that they'd recognise you if you did.'

'I'd have to think about it. This couldn't be a career for life, could it?'

'Not for life, but if you keep your looks, we get requests for women in their late fifties. There's a pension plan and you could save. You'd be able to retire comfortably by the time you were fifty-five.'

'How about friends and relatives?'

'Is that a problem for you?' Selena asked. 'If it is, don't tell them. We aren't going to put a sign up.'

'You've got it all worked out.'

'We think so. While you think, there's someone we'd like you to meet.'

They went down one floor and knocked on a door. Tina opened it. Connie and Tina threw themselves into each other's arms, squealing.

'You work here?' Connie asked.

'Sure do. This is the promotion I told you about. I couldn't tell you more back then.'

'You work on camera?'

'Part-time. I also do the wardrobe, wigs and makeup, if you like. *Do* come on board. It'd be more fun than being a – what is it – actuary?'

On her way back home, a few things became clear to Connie. She'd gone to the boutique and asked for the sexiest they had. Chances were, that had been Tina's cue to call Rupert. And then he and Selena just happened to show up at the pool, right outside her suite. It made sense. Where better to find exhibitionists to recruit than at the Gran Playa Aphrodite?

186

Chapter Twenty-one

Connie explained the offer she'd had to Shirley, over lunch. 'What do you think?' she asked.

'Five to ten grand a week, for showing off your bod, guaranteed "look-no-touch", working with at least three people who you already like and are really compatible with, right?'

'Yes,' Connie agreed, uncertainly.

'Do they have any vacancies?'

'What?'

'Do you know what our company pays receptionists? If your friends will take me, I'd jump at the job.'

Connie arranged an interview for Shirley, who was accepted. That meant that Connie's four best friends were in, so what else could she do?

The two girls spent their last afternoon at the office going round saying goodbye and avoiding answering questions about where they were going. Come five, Connie still hadn't bumped into Jeff. She needed to see him one last time, just for closure.

She asked and was told, 'Jeff? Didn't you know? He quit a week ago.'

Oh. Well, that settled it. All ties with the past were cut. She was truly launched into a whole new future.

Or adrift in one?

Chapter Twenty-two

Rupert's voice came over the speaker. 'Missy C and Zsa-Zsa, promo number one, take three. Sound, action, all that stuff.'

Connie walked towards the camera swinging her hips in her imitation pleated skirt and her 'stays on because it's glued' shirt. She paused where there was a duct tape cross on the floor and did a pirouette, clockwise. Her skirt stayed down, but swirled a little.

'Hi, guys!' She waved her fingers at the camera. 'I'm Missy C. Do you like my skirt? Short, isn't it? You like the way it shows my thighs off? Well, how about this?' She twirled counter-clockwise. Air got under her mock pleats and lifted them to the level of her waist for a fraction of a second. 'Did you see my pussy?' she asked. 'Am I wearing a thong, or nothing?' She spun again, faster. 'Catch it? Not sure? You want to be sure? Come and see me on Friday, if you do, 10 p.m. Central Time. I can wear this skirt for you, or maybe I won't, no skirt, just the shirt. You get to choose. Just press "N" for "No" if you want me to be bare below, "Y" if you want the skirt on, OK? Don't worry. Whichever wins, you *will* get to see my bare bum, and more, much more.' Connie beckoned off-camera. Shirley came on wearing just a carefully arranged satin sash.

Connie continued. 'This is my friend, Zsa-Zsa.' Connie hid her mouth with the back of her hand. 'Zsa-Zsa is coming to visit me on Friday. That's a bonus, right? What she doesn't know is, I've had the hots for her ever since we met. Friday, I've decided, I'm going for it. Zsa-Zsa, on my bed, doing every damn thing I can think of to her, and I've got a hell of an imagination. Even so, if there's anything special you'd like to watch me do to this lovely girl, or her to me, there's a 900 number at the bottom of your screen so you can dial your suggestions in. You can suggest *anything*. If I choose your idea, you get a session of viewing, free, on me. I'll make it good for the winner, I promise.

'So it's up to you, guys and girls, do I wear my skirt or not? And what do Zsa-Zsa and I do to each other? Your choice.' She leaned in close to blow a kiss at the camera. 'See you on Friday, 10 p.m. I'll be there. I'll be bare.'

'Cut,' Rupert called.

When he came into the room, Connie asked, 'How did we do, Rupert?'

'Irresistible. We got a good take.' He turned his head towards the open door. 'Good take, right?'

A voice called back, 'Perfect, but how else could it be, with Connie in it?'

Connie was struck dumb. A long jeans-clad leg stepped into the room. The rest of the man was covered by his shoulder-rig camera, which was aimed at her.

'Jeff?' she squeaked.

He put his rig down. 'Connie.'

'You? You know what we do here? What I've been doing?'

'I'm the only techie, and the cameraman. I've been your unseen admirer ever since you started work.'

'You don't mind? You aren't ashamed of me?'

'Because you do what I kept on at you to do? Of course not. I've been known to do a little performing myself, as it happens.'

'But ...'

He took her into his arms.

Rupert said, 'Our work here is done,' as he hustled Shirley out of the room. Over his shoulder, he called back, 'Don't forget to turn your cameras off before you forget in the heat of passion, you two.'

Jeff and Connie broke off their kiss for long enough for them both to say, 'Not on your life. We want to watch this, later, and you lot are all invited to the viewing.'

www.ingramcontent.com/pod-product-compliance
Ingram Content Group UK Ltd.
Pitfield, Milton Keynes, MK11 3LW, UK
UKHW022301180325
456436UK00003B/177